BLACK IS THE COLOR OF LOVE:
Eight Outstanding Short Stories about Generational Love

BLACK IS THE COLOR OF LOVE:
Eight Outstanding Short Stories about Generational Love

Frederick Williams
Editor

Jaed Publications
Los Angeles, California

JAED PUBLICATIONS
LOS ANGELES, CALIFORNIA

ISBN: 978-0-9709957-7-3

Inside text design: TWA Solutions and Services

Book Cover Design by Avista Products

Photo on Cover Provided by Adger Cowans

Printed in the United States of America

Dedication:

To the memory of Leslie David Perry, a great story teller, a lover of his culture and a man who refused to sacrifice his principles in his art.

ACKNOWLEDGMENTS

Most important is that I acknowledge my God, my Creator, who makes all things possible. This anthology about love is inspired by His love for all of us. I also must express my heartfelt thanks to the writers who heard my plea that we must create a series of short stories that express the positive nature of our people. That is exactly what Caleb Alexander, Lenton Collins, D.L. Grant, Leslie Perry, Margaret Richardson, Michael Smith and Antoinette Winstead did when they put pen to paper and created these outstanding stories. Thank you, my fellow artists, for a great job.

I also send a special thank you to Jessica Tilles of TWA Solutions and Services for taking my manuscript and editing and converting it to the appropriate software for publication. If you are a writer struggling with how to get your rough draft manuscript to a clean copy ready for the printer, I suggest you contact Ms. Tilles. I want to acknowledge Carl Booker of Avista Products for designing the cover and Adger Cowans for allowing us to use one of his many outstanding photographs on the cover.

On behalf of all the writers of *Black is the Color of Love,* we want to send a special appreciation to Dr. Camille Cosby for taking the time out of her very busy schedule to read our works and to also write a very encouraging foreword for us. It was the frosting on the cake.

Finally, I want to thank my wife, Venetta, who has always been by my side as I have taken on many projects regarding the beauty, strength, and endurances of the Black culture in this country. She represents the true essence of Black Love.

CONTRIBUTING AUTHORS

Caleb Alexander is a successful *New York Times* bestselling author and ghostwriter, responsible for some of the biggest titles in the Urban Fiction genre. Recognizing he wanted to change the genre of his writing, he abruptly decided to write stories of hope and uplift, publishing three works: *Eastside*, *Two Thin Dimes*, and *Belly of the Beast* that contributes valuable lessons for our youth. His short story, "The Gift," represents one of the best-written works in the anthology. It is a well-crafted story about the importance of family and heritage for the success of our youth.

Lenton Collins served a four-year tour in the United States Navy and is presently working in San Antonio, Texas, with the underground music scene. He is also a freelance writer, specializing in the rap music field. He has teamed with Margaret Richardson to write the moving and beautiful short story about the love shared between an elderly Black couple. The story is told from the voice of the couple's grandson.

D.L. Grant is the assistant branch manager of the George Washington Carver Branch Library in San Antonio, Texas, and is working on his doctorate in Library and Information Sciences. He is a member of the American Library Association and is the chair-elect of the Black Caucus of the Texas Library Association. He was recently elected to the Executive Board of the Black Caucus of the American Library Association and is also a member of the Beta Phi Mu Library and Information Studies Honor Society. He was awarded the President's Call to Service Award, presented by President Barack Obama's Council on Service and

Civic Participation. His short story tells of a young, fourteen-year-old boy's determination to get a library card from the local library in the segregated South.

Leslie Perry was a modern-day Griot for over thirty years and performed throughout his home state of California and many other states. He was a shaker and mover in the storytelling community in the greater Los Angeles area and was a founding member of the Los Angeles Storytelling Festival. Long before his life as a storyteller, Leslie was a theatre man and, among his creative works, was a performance of Frederick Douglass' famous Fourth of July speech. His one-act play *History Man* was performed at the University of Texas at San Antonio during Black History Month in 2009. Leslie published a series of short stories and a play entitled, *The Story Man*. In this anthology, Leslie has three folk tales, usually performed in a storytelling format, but changed to written format. His folk tales include: "Door of No Return," "Sunshine and the Gummy Man," and "Stone Gumbo Soup," and his short story is "A Time Remembered."

Margaret Richardson is a local scholar who has recently received her Master's Degree from the University of Texas at San Antonio in Political Science. She was awarded a Ruth Jones McClendon internship to work in the Texas State Legislature 2005 and worked on the staff of State Representative Jose Menendez. Margaret has written a beautiful short story that brings tears to your eyes. "Passing the Torch" is about the love shared by a couple that lasted for over fifty years, and it is told from the voice of their grandson. In her story, she points out the importance of family, heritage, and culture.

Michael Smith lived an exciting but dangerous life in the past. He worked as an undercover agent for a major police force in an East Coast city. After years of doing this work, Michael was bothered by the number of innocent people who happened to be at the wrong place at the wrong time and were taken down just like the criminals. He watched as the guilty cut deals with the district attorney's office and walked away with no time served if they agreed to turn snitch, while others with no significant involvement in the drug trade had their lives destroyed. Michael has used his experience as an undercover agent to write the novel, *Pieces of a Broken Man*, published in 2011. Excerpts from the novel are included in the anthology under the title, "Losing the Game."

Frederick Williams is the author of five published novels: *The Nomination, Beyond Redemption, Just Loving You, Fires of Greenwood: The Tulsa Riot of 1921*, and *Bayard and Martin: A Historical Novel About Friendship and the Civil Rights Movement*. He has ghostwritten five autobiographies and is the editor of the anthology, *Black is the Color of Love*. He recently completed a screenplay, *Defending Black Wall Street*, for a film bringing to the screen the great accomplishments of Black Americans on Black Wall Street in Tulsa, Oklahoma, and the hate that destroyed it on June 1, 1921. He is presently working on his sixth novel, *Making My Way to Harlem*. He is the Executive Editor of Jaed Publications LLC and President of Pairee Film Productions LLC. Williams invites you to visit his writer's blog at www.thewriterfred.com.

Antoinette Winstead, a poet, fiction writer, playwright, director, and actor earned a BFA in Film and Television Production from New York University and an M.F.A. in Film from Columbia University. Her poetry and short stories have been published in various magazines and anthologies. Her plays have been performed at the 24th Street Theater, Jump Start, The Steven Stoli Playhouse, the San Pedro Playhouse, the Carver Cultural Center, and the Overtime Theater. She teaches film and theater courses at Our Lady of the Lake University in San Antonio,

Texas, where she is a tenured full-Professor, and currently serves as the Associate Dean of the College of Arts and Sciences.

CONTENTS

THREE SHORT TALES AS TOLD BY
Griot Leslie Perry

FOREWORD

A very profound person gave me indelible advice at the onset of my doctoral field work…to elicit human's thoughts and feelings. Each of the author's work in, *Black is the Color of Love*, did just that.

I love the thread of commonalities within the anthology; that is, the sociological, historical truths about African Americans… and the importance to know those truths. Moreover, to have unity with loved ones, that is essential to healthily navigate America's relentless institutional and personal actions of vicious hatefulness against African Americans.

All eight short stories have clear messages of positiveness. One of my favorite scholars of African and African American histories, Dr. John Henrik Clarke wrote: "The cruelest thing slavery and colonialism did to the Africans was to destroy the memory of what they were before foreign contact."

Each author of the short stories has countered that ancient and ongoing abuse so astutely.

— Camille Cosby, Ph.D.

Introduction

In James Weldon Johnson's preface of *The Book of American Negro Poetry,* he writes, "The final measure of the greatness of all peoples is the amount and standard of the literature and art they have produced. The world does not know that a people is great until that people produced great literature and art. No people that has produced great literature and art has ever been looked upon by the world as distinctly inferior."

If you accept Johnson's premise of what makes a people great, then our literature must be one of the two most valued quantity within our race. Each of the writers in this anthology, *Black is the Color of Love,* has accepted the challenge to write a short story that meets the standards of greatness, established by one of our greatest writers over one hundred years ago. It was my honor to take on the responsibility to edit these wonderfully written short stories, and I have to admit, my job was rather easy.

This anthology is a continuation of the history of Black writers creating stories reflecting on the culture and heritage of the Black race. From Charles Chestnutt at the turn of the 20th Century through the Renaissance writers—Langston Hughes, Zora Neale Hurston, Dorothy West, Claude McKay—Blacks have specialized in the art or writing short stories. Based on a contemporary view of our culture, these eight stories accentuate the love, strength, and great tradition of Black America. The title reflects on the meaning of these works. Black love for family, friends, and community defines who we are. These writers from all different backgrounds and professional careers take pride in submitting their stories wrapped in that love for readers, young and old, to enjoy.

The first short story, "Scottie's Journey," is about a young, fifteen-year-old boy who discovered, after not making his high school basketball team, there is more to his life than a sport. He travels back in time to meet some of the great heroes of his race and learns from them that very lesson.

"The Gift," written by one of the best Black writers in this country, Caleb Alexander, is a brilliantly written story about a gift that binds a family together and is the source of their outstanding success in life. It opens the eyes of a young doctor to recognize how important one's heritage is to their success.

"In Perpetuity," the third story, takes a young boy back in history to experience the anguish and pain his ancestors suffered at the hands of an evil force, convincing him his behavior in no way should add any credence to the suffering of the past.

Michael Smith's "Losing the Game," carries a very important message about the legal system and how it is structured in such a way that no matter how good you may think you are, you cannot beat the long arm of the law.

"A Time to Remember," by the late Leslie Perry, tells the story of an older Black man on his way to vote in the 2008 election. On the way, he recalls all the hard times and the turmoil Blacks had to endure to finally get to the place in life they could vote for a Black man for president and the best part, he actually does get elected.

Antoinette Winstead's "Friday Night Wagon Wheel" raises the question: What can be so dangerous about an innocuous game called Wagon Wheel? Everything, if you are a young, Black boy on Friday night in East Texas, as reporter Alexandria Stevens discovers within the pages of this thrilling short story.

Introduction

"Passing the Torch," written by Professor Margaret Richardson and the late Lenton Collins, is a beautiful story about the love a family has shared through generations, and how their rich heritage is passed down from grandfathers to sons and grandsons.

District Director of the Carver Branch of the San Antonio Public Library, D.L. Grant, takes us on a trip back in time in his well-written short story, "One Boy's Quest for Knowledge," a time when even libraries were segregated. Young Levi Flood is determined to get a library card and refuses to be denied until finally he wins out.

These short stories are meant to add to the rich history of Black America that was hidden within the dark cloud of racism, bigotry, and hatred. However, over the past one hundred years, that history has been captured by writers from all over the country. This anthology is the San Antonio, Texas, writers' contribution to that literature.

Scottie's Journey

Frederick Williams

Monday morning couldn't come fast enough for fifteen-year-old Scottie Brown. When the alarm clock rang at 6:00 a.m., he sprang from his bed and rushed to the bathroom. Scottie lived in a two-bedroom apartment in a public housing unit off Fair Oaks Avenue in Pasadena, California. He shared a small bedroom with his younger brother, Alex. His mother, Wanda, occupied the bedroom on the other side of the apartment. They lived off Wanda's welfare check because there was no child support from Scottie's father, who abandoned the children right after Alex's birth. Despite their financial struggles, the family maintained a positive attitude about life, something Wanda insisted on. At some point, she knew she would get off welfare and move her family into a home in a better part of the city. Scottie was determined to help her and that's why this day was so important to him.

He had to beat his younger brother to the bathroom so he could wash up and be out of the apartment by seven. He noticed his mother's bedroom door still closed. She was sleeping later than her usual five o'clock wake up, something she would often do if she had gotten in late from her part-time job. Scottie closed the bathroom door, stripped out of his underwear, and poured the hot water in the bathroom sink. He splashed water over his upper body and face, then grabbed a towel and patted himself dry.

Scottie turned and stared at his physique in the full-length mirror on the back of the bathroom door. His five-foot-six-inch frame was slim but muscular. He'd shaved all the hair from his head, just like the professional basketball players did. All he wanted to do in life was play basketball, and he modeled his appearance after his favorite players who all had clean-shaven heads. The only missing symbol was the earring. His mother insisted he did not wear one and that he not get his ears pierced. But once he made his high school basketball team and she saw all the other players with pierced ears and earrings, she'd come around. That's why he had to hurry and get to school so he could learn the outcome of last week's tryouts for the school's basketball team.

He slipped on his underwear and hurried back to the bedroom where Alex sat on the side of his bed.

"What position you think they going to let you play?" Alex asked.

"Don't jinx me," Scottie shouted. "I ain't made the team yet and you talking like that might bring me bad luck." Scottie scolded his brother for jumping the gun even though he knew darn well there was no way he wouldn't make the cut. He had two great practices and no one looked better than he did in front of the coaches.

"Oh, man, you ain't got to worry. Can't none of them dudes throw up the ball like you can. You a shoo-in. I can't wait to come to your games.

"We'll see." A big smile spread across Scottie's face. "You'd better get ready before Mamma comes in here." Scottie watched his brother head toward the bathroom as he put on his FUBU sweats and jersey. He again glanced at his physique in the mirror, and then slipped into his Nike tennis shoes. He was now ready to take on the day.

When he entered the kitchen, Wanda stood over the stove preparing bacon and eggs for him, but he shot right by her and toward the front door.

"Where you going, boy?" she asked without looking his way.

"Mamma, I ain't hungry this morning."

"What you mean, you ain't hungry? You'd better get back over here and eat this food that I got out of the bed to fix you," Wanda scowled.

Scottie stopped and sauntered back to the kitchen table. Wanda placed his plate on the table in front of him.

"What are you in such a hurry for anyway?" she asked, taking a seat across from him at the table.

"I'm just in a hurry, Mamma. Scottie got up and hurried over to the refrigerator to get a glass of milk. He then returned to the table and started gulping down his food.

"Slow down, boy. What's wrong with you? I ain't ever seen you in this much of a hurry to get to school. You found some young girl that's got you all twisted?"

"No way, Mamma. Today they tell us who made the basketball team for this year."

"Boy, don't get your hopes all built up around a game," Wanda admonished. "I wish you could get just as excited about your grades as you are about a game."

"Mamma, I'm gonna go pro and get us out of here. You just wait and see."

"Whatever happens, just remember your mamma loves you and I want you to be a good student as well as a good ballplayer. You understand?"

"Yes, Mamma." Scottie pushed his plate away. "I'm finished so can I go now?"

"After you put that plate in the sink and rinse it off. You boys act like you got a maid around here."

Scottie got up and strolled over to Wanda. He kissed her on the cheek and then placed his dishes in the sink. "Okay, I'm gone now and you going to be real proud of me when I get home."

"I'm proud of you anyway."

After closing the apartment door, Scottie jumped down the steps, taking three at a time, until he got to the first floor of the apartment building. He then pushed open the door to the building and stepped out in the California morning sunshine. As he headed for the street, he ran into John Ambrose, the manager of the complex as well as one of the coaches at the local boys club where Scottie learned to play basketball. He had the utmost respect for his coach and mentor, John, who had been a great athlete at John Muir High School in Pasadena. Scottie thought of him as a surrogate father, a replacement for the one he'd never known.

"Hey, Uncle John," Scottie shouted. "This is the big day."

"Oh yeah, you find out your fate, don't you?" John placed his arm around Scottie's shoulder and walked next to him.

"It's going to be on now, Uncle John. Me and my boys going to kick somebody's butt in the conference."

"Don't get ahead of yourself," John admonished. "Check the list first and then celebrate when you see your name there."

"My name will be there. I tore them suckers up during tryouts."

John removed his arm from around Scottie's shoulder and stood there. "Just remember someone else makes that decision and basketball isn't everything in life. It's just a game."

"It was for you, Uncle John."

"Yeah, but I never went pro and I made sure I got a halfway decent education. Just think, if I had concentrated on school instead of ball and finished my college education, I'd be Director of the Boys Club by now instead of just the assistant. Keep that in mind, young brother." John gave Scottie a tight hug. "Remember, ball isn't everything. You have so many more things to accomplish in life. Don't limit yourself." He headed back inside the building.

Scottie stood motionless as he watched Uncle John enter the manager's office to the building. What if his name wasn't on the list? That couldn't be possible. He'd kicked too much butt in the tryouts not to make the team. Sure, he'd missed a few shots and one of the boys had scored at will over him. He still looked good and, anyway, his life would be over if his name was not on the list. Determined he'd be reporting to practice that afternoon, he turned and started up Fair Oaks Avenue to catch the bus to school.

When the bus pulled up in front of John Muir High School, Scottie jumped from his seat. He pushed his way by a number of other students, bolted off the bus, and headed for the gym.

"Hey, Scottie man," a young brother walking out of the gym shouted to him.

"Not now," Scottie shouted back. "I got to check out what's happening." He ran right by the brother and up the steps into the gym.

"But what I wanted to tell you was—"

Scottie slammed the door closed and didn't hear what the brother tried to tell him. He ran down the hall to the gym and swung the locker room door open. He spotted a half-dozen boys standing around a window that had a paper taped to it. Scottie watched as a couple of the boys, who'd been pretty good in practice, slapped hands, did a high-five and patted each other on the back. Apparently, they had made the team. Suddenly, they stopped celebrating as he approached them. Something was wrong. He slowed down, as he got closer to the window. The other boys said nothing to him. It felt like a ton of gravel pulled at his heart and Scottie's legs went weak as he looked at the twelve names of the players who'd made the junior varsity basketball team. He looked again and then a third time and a fourth time. Tears welled in his eyes. His name was not on the list.

The young boy, who had scored all over him in the tryouts, said, "Sorry, dawg, but you can always try out next year." He and the other two boys turned and walked away.

"Too bad, Scottie, but there's always next year," one of the other young brothers added. He turned and strolled up the stairway, leaving Scottie alone and crying inside.

The day dragged on forever. It seemed like the entire freshman class offered their condolences to him. With each student that approached him, he slid further down in his chair and deeper into his state of depression. He was a failure, and now his life meant very little to him. How could he possibly tell his mother, Uncle John, and his younger brother that he didn't make the team?

When the bell rang and his last class for the day was over, he hurried back down the stairs and stood outside the gym. He stared through the window and watched as the twelve players chosen for the team lined up and began shooting lay-ups. Again, his eyes filled with tears as he finally turned and walked away. He was in no hurry to go home, but at some point, knew he would have to deliver his disappointing news to his family. He still had time to catch the last bus, so he rushed to the front of the school and climbed aboard. This would be the longest ride of his life.

Scottie ran past Uncle John's apartment, rushed up the stairs and into the apartment. He could hear Tupac's "AllEyez on M*e*," and that meant Alex was in the bedroom. He couldn't face his little brother who thought the world of him. Alex considered his older brother an all-star who someday would be as good as Michael Jordan. Now he had to tell him that he didn't even make the junior varsity team. But he just didn't have to do it right then.

He swung the bedroom door open and Alex looked up at him from his bed where he was stretched out listening to the rap song. Scottie tried to ignore him. He went to his side of the room and fell out on his bed. He could detect Alex's eyes on him, and he knew what was coming.

"Well, don't keep me in suspense," Alex said. "Did you make the team?"

Scottie turned his back to him.

"Come on Scottie tell me, you going to be playing point guard or shooting guard? Or maybe they put you right on the varsity team?"

"Naw, they didn't put me on varsity."

"That's okay, 'cause you can really shine playing junior varsity. You better than all those chumps put together."

"I ain't better than nobody," Scottie snapped. "So just leave me alone. I'll tell you what happened later."

Alex jumped from his bed and turned the music off. "You ain't got to bite my head off," he said and walked out the door. "Way you actin', don't sound like you even made the team." He slammed the door behind him.

Scottie lay there staring at the ceiling. How could God be so cruel to him? He had given him a rotten father who never came around to see him and as far as he knew, never sent any money to help his mother. That's why she had to work all the time doing menial jobs so they could make ends meet. Now God had denied him the one dream he really wanted to come true. That was to be a great basketball star, make plenty of money, and then move his mother into a better house and neighborhood. Someplace where they wouldn't hear neighbors fighting all the time and hear shooting right outside their windows. Now that would never happen because he had no other ability or talent. Like his buddies, it was basketball or nothing. So, for him, it would be nothing.

****

Scottie didn't know if he had fallen asleep and captured the images that appeared in a dream or if they were real. Suddenly, Uncle John stood before him, but he was dressed differently. He looked like some kind of psychic or holy man. It scared Scottie and he drew back when Uncle John sat on the side of his bed. He placed his large hands on Scottie's shoulder.

"So, little brother, you didn't make the team."

Scottie froze up; he knew Uncle John would be angry with him. But the tone in his voice was soothing and reassuring. He tried to speak, but the words wouldn't come.

"Don't try to say anything," Uncle John admonished. "My last words to you this morning was to let you know things may not be as you want them to be. Don't be discouraged. I want to take you on a journey. And when we return, you'll reconsider your entire life and the feeling that you are a failure because you didn't make the basketball team. Now close your eyes, take my hand, and journey out into the world from which you came centuries ago."

Scottie trusted Uncle John, so, without hesitation, he reached out and grabbed his mentor's large, strong hand. Instantly, he felt his body moving but knew he was still lying in bed. He experienced a smooth, fast, and relaxing movement. The pace continued to increase and he felt the distance between his reality and the world to which they traveled.

"Wait, wait," Scottie screamed. "Where are we, Uncle John? Where are we and what's happening?"

"Trust me and relax," Uncle John whispered. "Just feel the bright light and let it take over."

The faster and further they went the brighter the light. Scottie closed his eyes and enjoyed the exhilarating feeling of existence outside of his physical body. They were caught up in the center of a light that was warm and non-threatening. Suddenly, they descended toward the ground. He had no idea where they landed. From what he'd seen in books at school, it appeared to be some kind of farm or plantation. He stared off to his left and there was a large white house with pillars out front, a beautiful green lawn, and a carriage off to the left side. To the right, several men were sitting atop horses with rifles in their hands. They took off riding toward the woods.

"Uncle John, where are—"

"Ssh. We can't make any noise or those men over there will take us in and we'll never get back to Pasadena." Uncle John pointed in the direction of the men who had just taken off riding toward the wooded area.

Scottie took Uncle John's warning seriously. "Where are we?" he whispered.

"We're back in time. The year is 1831 and we're on a plantation in Virginia." Uncle John led him around the side of the big white house.

When they reached the back, Scottie saw rows and rows of old beat-up wooden cabins without windows. There was no green grass, only dirt all around them. Chickens, along with some pigs and a couple of straggly looking dogs, wandered from cabin to cabin as if looking for scraps of food.

They approached the second cabin in the first row and Uncle John swung the door open. They both stepped inside and Scottie saw three Black men sitting on the dirt floor. One of the men jumped to his feet and pulled out a knife. He was a big muscular, dark-skinned man, with thick coarse hair and fire burning in his eyes. Scottie thought, *What a powerfully good-looking, strong Black man.* The kind of man they never saw in their history books. He must have put the fear of God in white people. No wonder they needed the extra advantage of guns and numbers to subdue men like the strong Black man standing in front of him.

"We mean no harm," Uncle John said. "This boy comes to you because he has a few questions for the revolutionary prophet Mr. Nat Turner."

"What is it you want with me?" Nat asked in a deep and commanding voice.

"Prophet Nat, this boy is concerned about his future. You see, in his time era, many of our young brothers are more concerned about honing their basketball skills, a sport where people throw a ball into a net, instead of their learning skills. A test of a young man's worth in some of our communities is how well he plays a game. So, Scottie thinks—"

"What is this basketball?" Nat interrupted. "Is it something needed to fight our oppressor for our freedom? Will it help to defeat him?"

"No, sir," Uncle John said with humility. "What you're about to do will eventually lead to a war that will end slavery. So, this boy lives in a free world and his only concern is that he be able to play this game better than the other boys. He feels that his world will crumble if he doesn't win at this game."

"A game," Nat shouted. He turned and stared at the other two men. He then walked over to Scottie and placed his hand on the boy's shoulder. "Young brother, these men and I are getting ready to go to our death tonight, fighting for Black folks' freedom. Does your game help free Black people in your world? Does it benefit the race or just the individual? That game will someday be forgotten, just like it is not known to us now, but what we do here tonight will be remembered forever. Forget that game and go back to your place in time and do something to help your people. Don't let our deaths be in vain." Nat ended his words of wisdom and waved his arms back and forth.

Scottie felt his body caught up in the power of Nat Turner and it lifted Uncle John and him right out of the cabin and back into the bright light of time. Again, he felt his body floating through space to a different part of the country, but still one filled with danger. Scottie could see a heavily wooded area with no houses or roads. As they started down into the dark of night, he saw a campfire with ten Blacks, all dressed in raggedy clothes, huddled around the fire for warmth. He knew the leader of the group was the Black woman with a red bandanna around her head and a pistol in her hand. She appeared to be fussing with one of the others in the group. Scottie and Uncle John landed right next to the woman. She jumped back and aimed her pistol at both of them.

"Wait, Mrs. Tubman," Uncle John pleaded. "Please don't shoot. We come from another time era, seeking your advice."

"What is it that you want with me and my people?" Harriet scowled. "I just got these folks this morning off the Peabody plantation outside Natchez, Mississippi. We got a long ways to go to freedom. And our enemy already done put the slave hunters and them dogs on our trail. So, what is it you want? Hurry, man. We don't have much time." Harriet glared at Scottie. "Well, what is it, boy? What do you need to know?"

Uncle John spoke up. "Mrs. Tubman, we come from the time-space of 2019. Your tireless work and bravery in bringing Blacks to freedom have since helped to do away with slavery. This boy comes from a free world, so he thinks. His biggest concern is that he didn't make the basketball team, a sport at his school."

"School for Black children?" Harriet shrieked. "You hear that, my fellow brothers and sisters? This boy goes to a school." She now turned and glared at Scottie. "Why are you so concerned about this team? Is making this team more important than learning to read and write, something these beautiful people have been deprived of all their lives? They'd sacrifice their life if they knew their kids could learn to read and write someday in the future. On the plantation, we aren't allowed to do those things. Our enemies are scared that if we know how to read, then we can study about the great Nat Turner's sacrifice he made years ago for us." Harriet suddenly stopped talking as they heard a twig snap in the woods. "Everyone quiet," she whispered.

Scottie felt a shiver run through him. What if he got caught with the others? Would he ever be able to return to his time frame? He was beginning to get a better understanding of what his ancestors went through at the hands of an evil and brutal system of oppression. He watched as Harriet crept over to the area where they heard the sounds. She checked it out with pistol drawn, no doubt ready to be used if necessary. As he followed her every move, he recalled one of his teachers telling the class that oftentimes the slaves were very happy and content with their station in life and the slave owners were kind. Now, as he experienced the fear of oppression, he knew that was all one big lie.

After checking out the area where they heard the sound, Harriet returned to the spot next to Uncle John and Scottie.

"These people here will never give up their rights to be educated. That's why they risk their lives to escape from slavery, even with the white oppressors on their trail." She moved in closer to Scottie and stared directly into his eyes. "And you're worried about some game. Please don't tell me after all this struggle that our future generations going to worry about if they can play a game?"

Scottie was frozen in place. He felt ashamed, and knew he could do nothing but stand and listen.

"Boy, go back to your time and master the ability to read and write so you can continue the work we've started for our race's survival. Go help some Black folks, then you'll also help yourself. Now get out of here before you get caught and can't go back and do your job. Please tell our people that these monsters were never our masters. That is a lie they tell. We call them that for fear of severe beatings. But know that behind their backs, we call them exactly what they are, monsters and oppressors." Harriet clapped her hands and instantly, Scottie felt the air under Uncle John and him lifting and moving them forward in time and location.

The force carried them at such a rapid speed, Scottie had no idea where they would end up. He traveled through the dark and light with Uncle John by his side. He tried to talk, but words failed him. He finally closed his eyes and just waited for them to land at their next destination.

It didn't take long. They landed with a thud on the floor of what appeared to be a library or study in someone's home. Scottie lay flat on his back and when he rose on his side, he saw a light-skinned man with long, gray hair and a matching beard sitting at a desk surrounded by more books than he'd ever seen in his life. He had no idea Black men read that much. In his neighborhood, everyone watched television and listened to music. He also saw a bunch of newspapers, with the heading *North Star,* scattered on the floor. The man looked from his reading and writing at Scottie and Uncle John sitting on the floor.

It surprised Scottie when Uncle John called out the man's name.

"Mr. Frederick Douglass, please forgive us for this intrusion."

Frederick Douglass glowered at the two of them. Despite his fierce stare, Scottie felt attracted to the man. Douglass resonated a feeling of comfort and security. Scottie didn't want Uncle John to spoil that feeling by talking about basketball. He didn't want this man to think as the other two had, that his only concern was for himself. Scottie began to feel embarrassed because of his childish behavior when he found out he didn't make the team. That all seemed irrelevant now as he listened to Black men and women who did great things for Black people. To his chagrin, Uncle John did not spare him.

"Mr. Douglass, my young friend has been feeling low and depressed because he—"

"Don't tell me," Douglass interrupted. "He didn't make some kind of team and now he thinks his life is over."

"How did you know?" Scottie conjured up enough courage to ask.

"You've already visited with my friend Nat, who that same night you met with him struck a mighty blow for freedom. He'll live in the minds and hearts of Black folks forever. He'll be there even after your game is no longer around." Douglass stood up, sauntered over to the window, and stared out. The silence lasted for over a minute. He then returned to his chair, sat down, and crossed his legs. He stared directly at Scottie. "It's good to feel a passion for something. Just like Nat and Harriet, I feel a passion for freedom for my people." Suddenly Douglass raised his arm and brought his balled fist crashing down on the table. The noise startled Scottie, but he didn't fear this man.

"We have to be free in this century and we have to prosper in generations to come in the next centuries. Make no doubt about it, this is our country just like it is for any other group. Nat, Harriet, and I can help with the freedom, but you, young man, and your generation must help us prosper. I guess this game is going to help some, but what about the other millions of our people? What's going to happen to them while these few players prosper? Take that passion you have for this game and direct it toward your people. And you can help them only if you learn to work the white man's system. This game won't teach you how to do that. School and education will. I was forced to sneak to learn how to read. You can do it freely and with no restrictions except the one you impose on yourself. Understand what you have to do, young man, and go back to your time and direct that passion to benefit all the people and not just you."

"Thank you, Mr. Douglass," Uncle John said, as they got up and prepared to leave.

"What are you writing?" Scottie asked, as he also got to his feet.

"I am writing a Fourth of July speech that I will read on that historic day. I will, in my speech, point out the hypocrisy of this country that has the nerve to celebrate a day of freedom while keeping others in bondage. Hopefully, it will help serve the abolitionist cause against slavery. And, hopefully, someday you and your generation will read it and realize that we did not like slavery and were not happy in bondage. But first, you and your generation must learn to read before you can understand what we endured just for you."

With those final words, Scottie and Uncle John swooshed back out the door and into the time dimension. Now accustomed to the trip they were on, Scottie felt comfortable asking Uncle John about what was happening to them.

"How is this all happening, Uncle John?"

"We are traveling through the time funnel of the Black experience in this country. The totality of these experiences is what constitutes our culture. Each one of the individuals you have met did something of great importance to help build that culture that we all should be proud of, but just don't know a lot about."

"So, we are all connected through these experiences that go back way over a hundred years."

"Exactly, and they go back much further than that. They go all the way back to the continent of Africa when our ancestors were brought over here in the bottom of slave ships. They held on to many of the great achievements of their ancestors and then added the ones we have accomplished here in this country. That is what constitutes our culture. It is on loan to each new generation and it is their duty to preserve it, add something new and exciting and positive to it, and then pass it on to a generation after them."

"Amazing," Scottie mumbled, as they slowed down for the next visit.

This time they landed in a classroom with approximately thirty students sitting at desks, totally concentrating on every word spoken by the scholarly looking professor. Like Douglass, the man was light-skinned in color with a mustache and Van Dyke beard. The man appeared to be soft and warm.

Scottie and Uncle John scrambled to their feet and stood against the wall. All eyes were riveted on them. The professor spoke first.

"Young man, I see that you have been to see Nat, Harriet, and Frederick. How fortunate you are. These students study about them and you actually had the chance to meet them. What an honor."

"Who are you?" Scottie asked.

"What do you mean, who is he?" a number of the students shouted at Scottie. "Where have you been and what are you learning at your school? This is our leader and the greatest scholar in the country, Dr. W.E.B. Du Bois. He's the first Black man to receive a Doctorate Degree from Harvard University. He's teaching us here at Atlanta University how to understand the world so that someday the entire race can prosper and graduate from schools like Atlanta University and Howard University."

One of the young students wearing overalls and no shirt jumped to his feet and stuck out his chest. "He has designated us as the Talented Tenth with the enormous, but critical responsibility to go out and educate the rest of our race once we finish our studies. How well he does and how well we do depend on you all in the future. Have you all taken the same serious attitude about the Black race here in America as we have?"

Scottie began to feel intimidated by these young men. They were about his age, but only one hundred years earlier. Their commitment to the future of the Black race far surpassed any commitment coming from his friends at John Muir High School. Scottie wondered when and where had all this fervor been lost.

"Quiet," Dr. Du Bois admonished the class. He turned and stared at Scottie. "I know why you are here?"

"How do you know that?" Scottie asked in a somber tone.

"You're searching for your own way. You've been disappointed because you didn't make the basketball team at your high school."

"You know about basketball?" Scottie asked

"Yes, young man, I certainly do. In fact, I've thrown up a couple of hoops in my later life."

"Dr. Du Bois, what advice would you give Scottie about his future?" Uncle John finally asked.

"You see these young men in this room?" Du Bois pointed to the students. "They'll do anything to get an education because they know it will help them and it'll help the race. I tell you to stretch your mind and your imagination. Test the limits of your ability and when you feel you've reached that point, keep on going. Don't ever quit and be twice as good as the other race. Read, study, and understand that you are a part of a mighty people who know how to struggle and win. You can't do that just shooting hoops all day."

"I'm not sure I understand," Scottie said.

"Don't worry. It'll come to you in time. Here's a copy of my writings, *Soul of Black Folks*. Take it and study it." Du Bois handed Scottie a copy of the book. He then placed his hand on Scottie's shoulder. "Play your game for fun and exercise, young man. But read and study for your survival. Now you all must be on your way." Du Bois turned and sauntered back to his desk in front of the class. "I have squandered twenty minutes of these students' time and that's twenty minutes they must make up." Du Bois took his pointer and struck it against the blackboard. Scottie lifted off the floor and taken out of the room.

As they floated through space, Scottie and Uncle John could actually see days, weeks, and years pass by. The force carried them to a large hall with a podium up front and rows of seats lined up for the audience. A tall, thin man with flaming red hair, a short beard, and wearing black-rimmed eyeglasses stood in front of the podium and stared out at the crowd. Scottie and Uncle John took seats in the front row. The man spoke with fire in his voice.

"You just left Dr. Du Bois, a real scholar and a tribute to the Black race," the man said.

"Aren't you Malcolm X?" Scottie asked with excitement in his voice.

"Yes, I am, my young brother, and I am pleased you came to see me about your concerns. I assume by now, after visiting my fellow heroes of the race, you do realize you have a problem, but it can be resolved."

"How did you know?" Scottie asked, but this time he was pretty sure how the great man knew.

"We have quite a network set up for our communications between generations. We are worried about you and your many young brothers and sisters of the future."

"Excuse me, sir," Uncle John interjected. "This boy thinks that his life is over because he didn't make the basketball team at his high school."

"I know," Malcolm X said. "You count yourself fortunate, young brother, that your uncle has taken the time to save you from your own destruction. Basketball is right for some, but that number is so small that it is doing our race a disservice."

"What do you mean?" Scottie probed.

"You kids are buying the hype that the National Basketball Association is waiting to make you all superstars and super-rich. You see a few great players like Michael Jordan and Kobe Bryant, and the new young super phenom, Lebron James, and you think that's the life for you. Here is a statistic for you and it is right out of your time period." Malcolm paused and pulled a paper out from his inside jacket pocket. "For every five thousand boys who play junior high basketball, only five hundred play high school. And out of that five hundred, only fifty play college ball. Now, I'd say the chances of hitting it big are not good, but you have every young buck out there putting all their chips on making it to the pros. When they don't even make it to college, they got nothing, but maybe a chance to play ball on the concrete inside the prison." Malcolm X paused to let this message settle in with Scottie.

"While you are concentrating on basketball, they are busy building new prisons 'cause the man knows the real deal. He checks out attendance at inner-city schools so he'll have a good idea of how many prison beds he'll need in the future. Once you don't learn how to read, 'cause you're so busy playing ball, then you turn to crime. I know, 'cause I did." Malcolm spoke with emphasis.

He looked up at the crowd sitting patiently waiting for him to finish with Scottie so he could get on to addressing them. "It's okay to feel bad about not making your team, but you have to get over it and continue to pursue your studies. Read history and learn about your people. Study government so someday you can run the country. Learn mathematics so you'll be able to function in a technological world. If you can accomplish these disciplines, your pride and feeling of self-worth will far exceed any reward you get from playing a game. Now, I have a very important speech to deliver this evening, and you all must excuse me." Malcolm slapped his hands together, and Scottie, with Uncle John, took off on their way to the final destination of the journey.

They landed right at the front of the Lincoln Memorial in Washington, DC. It was midday and Scottie looked out at thousands of people standing around, evidently waiting for someone to speak. He then looked up at the steps of the Memorial. A number of men and women mingled around the microphone set up at the front of the stage. Suddenly, a man he knew from the history books and the picture in his grandmother's house hurried toward him.

"I only have a few minutes to talk with you," the man said.

"You're Dr. Martin Luther King, Jr., aren't you?" Scottie asked in astonishment.

"Yes, I am. In a few minutes, I have to address the multitude of people who want to know about our future. I have a dream I want to share with them. But before I do, let me share a private dream with you."

Scottie and Uncle John moved in closer to Dr. King so they could better hear every word spoken.

"My dream is that someday there will be no prisons to house our youth in such large numbers. My dream is that we will have more of our children born in two-parent families than those just in one-parent households. My dream is that someday, young Blacks like you will go to the library like you run to the basketball court. My dream is that there won't be any more crack houses and crack heads, heroin addicts, and, for that matter, any other drugs in our communities. My dream is that our hatred will be replaced with a love and respect for one another." Dr. King paused and took Scottie's hand. "Scottie, help me to make my dream come true. Return to your time and make a difference. Still play your basketball, but also play in the real game of life and that is for our survival." With those words, King disappeared, as did all the surroundings.

Scottie shot straight up in the bed. Uncle John sat next to him and his mother stood at the bedroom door.

"How you doing, young fellow?" Uncle John asked.

"I don't know. I had the weirdest dream." He glared at his mother and then at Uncle John. "You were in the dream with me, Uncle John, and we were on a trip and I met all these famous people."

"I know," Uncle John said. "And you now know what you have to do."

A big smile crossed Scottie's face. "I sure do."

"You think you can handle it?" Uncle John asked.

"Just watch me, because I know I got history on my side. I got so much to be proud of and to talk about that I can't wait to get to school in the morning."

"How about basketball?"

"It's just a game. Just basketball."

The Gift

Caleb Alexander

Dr. Shelby Cole stormed through the antiseptic-smelling halls of Johns Hopkins Medical Center, searching anxiously for a water fountain. She found one and drank incessantly, trying to quench her parched mouth and dampen her frustration.

"How could he?" she whispered.

Shelby clenched her teeth first, then her fist and pounded it against the off-white colored wall in front of her. *How could I have accepted?* she wondered.

"Shell, what's the matter?" a voice called out to her.

Shelby turned to see her friend, Dr. Holly Griffon, standing behind her.

"Nothing really," Shelby answered with a rush of air flowing out of her words.

"It didn't look like nothing just a few seconds ago."

Shelby raked her hand through her hair, sending it back over her shoulders. She couldn't hide the truth from Holly. They had been best friends and roommates all through undergraduate school at Spelman and then again at Howard Medical School, where they both studied to realize their dreams of becoming pediatricians. Holly knew her better than she knew herself.

"Dwight just invited me to spend Christmas with his family in Maine."

Holly crossed her thick arms and rested them lightly over her hefty midsection. She then leaned forward and engaged her friend with a raised eyebrow.

"And?"

"And I accepted."

"And?"

Shelby raised her arms, lifting her palms toward the ceiling. She shrugged her petite shoulders. "And…well…I don't think I'm ready for that yet."

Holly smacked her full, burgundy-colored lips and shook her head forcefully, causing her thick, gold hoop earrings to shake. "Girl, ready for what?"

"For that kind of commitment."

"He didn't ask you for your hand in marriage," Holly scowled. "He just asked you to spend Christmas with his family."

Shelby again raked her hand through her hair and blew out a breath of frustration. "You know how these things are. I mean, he's taking me to meet his family."

"Okay, let me get this straight." Holly ran her well-manicured finger through her small, perfectly round Afro. "Dwight Cheikh, eligible young bachelor, educated doctor, fine as all outdoors, nicer than the church house deacon, sweet as a stalk of Jamaican sugar cane, has asked you to go meet his family? Now, this is the same Dwight who sends you candy, cards, and flowers like they are going out of style? The same Dwight who calls you every night just to tell you how much you mean to him and how much he cares for you? Dwight, who every eligible female doctor, nurse, and technician in this hospital would die to have a man like?"

"Yes, like!" Shelby agreed. "But not Dwight. He's more like a good friend, close buddy type guy. The kind of guy that you call when it's snowing outside and you have a flat tire in the middle of the night."

"Oh yeah, good old reliable, dependable, trustworthy, faithful Dwight. Who would want a man like that?" Holly pursed her lips and tossed her head toward the ceiling. "Girl, what on Earth was I thinking?"

"You don't understand. Dwight's nice, he's sweet, but—"

"But what?"

"But… he's Dwight. No depth, no coordination, no fashion sense, no excitement, and no fire."

"Then let him go," Holly said flatly.

Shelby folded her arms and turned away from her friend. She took several steps down the hall before stopping and turning to face Holly. "You don't understand."

"Shell, what is it to understand?"

"I like Dwight. He's a good friend, a wonderful companion, a really sweet boyfriend, but—"

Holly raised her eyebrows, encouraging Shelby to continue.

"Let's just say Dwight's a BMW, but I want to marry a Ferrari. I want to be surprised. I want a little salsa, a little spice, and a little spontaneity. I don't think Dwight's capable of those things."

"Wrong! First of all, sweetie, salsa and spice will give you heartburn. Unless you want your heart to get burnt, you'd best stay away from those things. Second, you're running around looking for a Ferrari, when you already have a Rolls Royce. Dwight's not fast, maybe not even exotic, but he is rare, and he is the epitome of class. He's a good man. Girl, don't lose a bag of platinum, trying to go for a fist full of gold."

Shelby smiled. Somehow, Holly always knew the right things to say. It was her wisdom that got them through medical school and kept them out of trouble at Spelman.

Holly smiled back with a knowing smile, and ready arms because she knew what was coming next.

Shelby stretched out her arms and wrapped them around her friend. "Why do you always get to be right? Why can't I be right sometimes?"

"Oh, Shell, just do the right thing." Holly squeezed Shelby's petite frame. She stared into her friend's deep, chocolate brown eyes. "Remember the promise we made when we graduated from med school?"

"To listen to our patients?"

Holly nodded. "Uh-huh, that's one of them. Another was to always listen to our hearts. Listen to your heart, Shell. Don't go through life detached, neutral, and always analytical. Don't plan out every single thing that's ever supposed to happen to you."

"I don't do that," Shelby protested.

"Oh yeah you do, girl. I'll bet you know exactly what you want this mythical, salsa and spice, Ferrari man to be wearing when he comes to drive you off into the sunset."

They both laughed.

"So, don't rule out Mr. Dwight?" Shelby asked after they stopped laughing.

"What does your heart say?"

"I care about him a whole lot."

"Then go. Give him a chance."

"I guess you're right. I mean, it's not like I have any other big plans for Christmas."

Holly nodded and smiled. "Good."

Shelby slapped her hand against her forehead. "God, I hope he doesn't get up there and embarrass me."

"Embarrass you how, Shell?"

"I don't know…any number of ways. By dancing for one. Girl, you remember the last time we went to the club with him? He got up and started shaking his narrow butt, doing that old rhythmless herky-jerky dance that he does."

"Paging Dr. Griffon," the loudspeaker interrupted their conversation. "Paging Dr. Griffon. Please report to pediatrics."

While they walked down the hall, Holly started shaking and twisting convulsively. "Do the herky-jerky! Do the herky-jerky!" she sang as they turned the corner. "Do the herky-jerky!"

****

Shelby laid her head back on the headrest as Dwight pulled into a long driveway and proceeded to the front of a magnificent white Victorian-style mansion. Maine was beautiful in the winter. Snow-covered the grounds and was piled on the individual branches of the bare trees. The small stream that flowed along the side of the mansion was frozen solid, the white picket fence matched well with the snow, and the low, pink clouds in the sky looked like puffs of cotton candy. Smoke was coming from the chimney, indicating the fireplace was ablaze inside the mansion. It was simply Christmas-card beautiful as they pulled up and Dwight parked the car off to the left in the driveway.

As he got out of the car to come around and open the door for Shelby, Dwight spotted a small group of young adults helping a larger group of children build a round and robust snowman. He then gazed at the other cars parked in the cobblestone driveway. There was a Porsche, Range Rover, Navigator, and a Mercedes, all belonging to members of his family. The crew was all there and ready to celebrate the holiest of days.

The first person out to greet Dwight and Shelby was a young girl, bundled from head to toe in a soft pink Oshkosh snowsuit. Dwight opened his arms wide to receive her.

"Meghan." Dwight took her by the arms and lifted her high into the air.

"Uncle Dwight," the young girl giggled.

Dwight managed to spin Meghan through the air once, and then found himself surrounded by the rest of the troupe.

Shelby laughed and smiled uncontrollably as she watched Dwight descend to one knee and pass out hugs and kisses like candy. He obviously was one of the family favorites. She saw four other young women run out of the house and right up to Dwight. She figured they were family.

"Dwight," the first young lady shouted.

Dwight hugged each of the four and then turned to Shelby. He grabbed her hand and pulled her close to him. "Shell, I'd like you to meet my sister, Stephanie, my sister, Erykah, my cousin, Sydney, and my cousin, Terri. Hey, y'all, this is Dr. Shelby Cole."

Shelby extended her hand to them, but was pulled into a series of embraces. Tight ones.

"It's good to finally meet you," Stephanie said.

"Dwight has told me so much about you. I feel like we're family already," Erykah said.

"Already, already!" The words bounced through Shelby's mind like a tennis ball at the Williams' sisters' home. She could still feel the force of them when Terri stepped forward and hugged her.

"Dwight talks about you all the time," Terri said.

Shelby felt she already knew Terri. She was not only Dwight's cousin but also one of his best friends. She held her hug a little longer than she did the others.

Sydney took her turn and leaned forward to hug Shelby. Her embrace was interrupted by a call from the front door of the farmhouse.

"You kids get in here before you catch a cold," said an elegantly dressed older woman, with a head of beautiful gray hair. She wore a long, pleated, forest green skirt that stopped just above her ankles to reveal a matching pair of suede boots. She also had on an oversized, multi-colored sweater with a Christmas motif that complimented her skirt and boots. Her ears were adorned with a set of pearls surrounded by tri-clustered diamonds. Her deep burgundy lips contrasted well with her pearlescent smile and her rich sandstone colored skin. But her most striking feature was the way she stood and moved with grace. An aura of dignity emanated from her very presence.

"Aunt Marjorie," Dwight said, as he approached the porch. "How is my ninth favorite aunt?"

"There are only eight of us," Marjorie said, as they embraced. "How is my twenty-first favorite nephew?"

"There are only twenty of us." Dwight smiled.

"Oh, well." Marjorie shrugged. "And who is this?" She looked at Shelby.

"Aunt Marjorie, this is my very close friend, Shelby." He placed his arm around Shelby. "This is my aunt Marjorie, Terri's mom."

Shelby extended her hand, but instead, Marjorie took her into another hug. Shelby wondered if this family ever heard of a handshake.

They broke their embrace. Marjorie stepped aside and waved her arm, inviting them inside. Shelby entered first, with Dwight right behind her.

As he passed by, Marjorie whispered in his ear, "Not bad, pumpkin. A little thin if you ask me, but not bad."

Shelby overheard Marjorie's comment. She wanted badly to turn around and say, "You're not so bad yourself, toots," but she resisted the urge.

Most of Dwight's family had gathered inside the exceptionally large living room. Shelby calculated its size and concluded that it was larger than her entire apartment back in Baltimore. A tall, brightly decorated tree stood majestically in the center of the room with plenty of beautiful decorations, and the massive, mahogany trimmed, brick fireplace, with logs ablaze, crackled off to the left. It was surrounded by dozens of bright red stockings. Shelby took in the pine mixed with burning logs from the fireplace. It smelled just like Christmas throughout the room. Two men and three women stood around the tree, drinking hot apple cider out of beautifully engraved glass cups.

The sounds emanating from the piano grabbed Shelby's attention. Several young adults had gathered around a Steinway Baby Grand, while one young lady played Stevie Wonder's "Ribbon in the Sky."

"Here," Dwight said, startling her. He handed Shelby what appeared to be a cup of eggnog.

"Thank you." She took the cup and sipped from it. "This is a lovely home," she said between sips.

"It's our family homestead. Been in the family for generations. Come on, I'll show you around and introduce you to everyone."

They strolled into the kitchen where a number of the women stood at the kitchen table, preparing the Christmas meal even though it was still a couple of days off. The aroma from the various foods teased Shelby and made her hungry. She wanted to eat right then and there. It always seemed to be the older women who were in charge when the food was being prepared. It was no different here. It reminded Shelby of the many Christmas celebrations she had spent at home with her family.

Dwight took her hand and led her over to an elderly lady sitting on a chair in the corner of the room. It seemed to Shelby that the woman's deep, rich, brown eyes penetrated right through her as she stood in front of the old lady.

"Shelby, this is my grand Dora. She is my great grandmother and she is one hundred one years old."

"Boy, don't be telling my age 'cause I still look like I'm young and only eighty." Dora's voice resonated across the room in sharp, unbroken tones of authority. She reached out to hug Shelby. "Where did this boy find someone as pretty as you, young lady?"

"Thank you, ma'am." *What an absolutely beautiful woman. I can't believe she is over one hundred years old*, she thought. "I work with your grandson at the hospital."

"You his nurse?" Dora asked.

"No, ma'am, I'm a doctor. I'm a pediatrician."

"Praise to Jesus, look what progress this race is making. We don't only have men doctors, which was the case in my day, we now got our women as doctors. I need another hug, honey."

Shelby hugged Dora one more time and they moved over to two ladies who looked quite alike with one appearing to be just a little older than the other. She especially noticed how the older lady was dressed in her long, pleated skirt, and suede boots. She wore a burgundy double-breasted top with double rows of pearl and diamond clustered buttons and a large burgundy and black paisley scarf hanging loosely over her left shoulder. The younger lady wore an elegant, navy-blue dress with double rows of gold buttons that accentuated her large, gold earrings, and gold bracelets that hung loosely around her wrist. She sported double rows across her hair in a twist and joined at the back forming a V. Shelby thought these ladies knew how to dress. The two ladies stood over the kitchen sink, cleaning a bunch of greens.

"Shelby, I want you to meet the other two ladies who are the most important in my life right now." Dwight placed his arm around the one who looked to be younger. "This is my mother,

Dr. Bernadette Cheikh, and this other gorgeous lady is my grandmother, Granny Grand."

The three ladies hugged and Dwight continued. "Shelby is my dearest of friends and is a pediatrician at the hospital."

"I heard you tell Grand Dora that," Bernadette said. "That's just wonderful. We ladies got it going on, don't we Shelby?"

"Yes, ma'am, we sure do," Shelby concurred and they all laughed.

The piano playing came to an end and was replaced with sounds from the radio. The Mighty O'Jays blared through the speakers singing, "Family Reunion." Dwight's sister, Erykah, his cousins Tracey, Terri, and Brittany, and his sister-in-law, Lauren, jumped up and started dancing. To Shelby's horror, Dwight joined them.

Shelby's hands flew to her face and covered her mouth in embarrassment as Dwight danced off beat with the others. Dwight's cousins, aunts, and everyone else in the room began laughing.

"Dwight, sit your no-rhythm-having butt down somewhere, boy," Aunt Connie shouted.

"Nope, and this is all your faults. Y'all sent me to boarding school in Canada, and so now you have to reap what you've sown." Dwight spun around and flailed his arms through the air like a spasmodic harem dancer. "So, now you have to watch, and eat your hearts out."

Dwight's dancing had everyone laughing, including himself.

Shelby felt good watching Dwight having a lot of fun. He couldn't dance, but that didn't stop him from enjoying himself. Shelby laughed so hard she developed a slight headache.

When they finally sat down, Dwight's dancing was the topic of conversation.

"Dwight, I'll never forget the time when we were in medical school at Meharry, and we all went out to the club," Terri said. She turned toward the rest of the family and Shelby. "Dwight got up to dance, and my goodness, he cleared the entire dance floor. Everyone just stood around watching him, like they were in shock."

"I remember that time," Brittany chimed in. "I was down there visiting with you all. And when Dwight started dancing, I didn't know whether to applaud or run for help."

"Hey, y'all," Bernadette shouted in her strong West Indian accent. "Stop teasing my baby boy. Him can't help it 'cause him don't have any rid-dem. You blame it on his far-der, not me." She was a thin lady, but had an overwhelmingly strong voice.

Shelby knew from conversations with Dwight that his mother had also attended Meharry along with his father. They met during medical school. There were so many successful people in this family. How did they do it? When she thought she had been sufficiently awestruck by this family's credential, what she learned next shocked her even more.

"Shelby, Dwight told us you're specializing in pediatrics?" Dwight's aunt Colleen asked.

"Yes, ma'am."

"Great," Aunt Colleen replied. "You know my husband and I are both pediatricians, and so are our daughters, Sydney and Robyn. If there's anything we can do to help you, don't hesitate to give us a call."

"Thank you," Shelby said somewhat tongue-tied. She turned to Dwight and asked, "Are all the members of your family doctors?"

"Just about." He smiled, as did the rest of the family. "All my aunts and uncles are doctors. I've got a couple of cousins who have Doctorates in Aeronautical Engineering, in Physics, and Economics. My cousin, who isn't here yet, is a lawyer. We just don't know how she went astray. Majoring in something outside the sciences."

"I'm very impressed," Shelby said. She then got up and stretched. "Dwight, could you show me where I'm going to be sleeping? That long drive up from Baltimore has just worn me out."

"Shame on you, Dwight," Bernadette interjected. "You should have already shown her to the special guest room overlooking the lake. I'm sorry, darling, but my son is not acting like a Cheikh. You'll get the opportunity to meet his father tomorrow, who is a real gentleman, you know from the old school. He would have been up here but had a late emergency at the hospital."

"I'm looking forward to it," Shelby said. "You all have quite a family."

"Come on, I'll show you where you can tuck away for the night." Dwight led Shelby out of the room.

"Good night, all. I'll see you in the morning." Shelby followed Dwight out of the living room.

"Good night, Shelby," the family said in unison.

Shelby lay in the bed with several troubling thoughts on her mind. Who were these people? Where did they come from and how did they all become so successful? What was their secret? She drifted off to sleep with that question burning in her mind.

That morning, Shelby woke up to a fantastic picture window view of the trees covered with snow and the lake frozen solid and also snowed over. It was a perfect view of nature at her best. She showered, dressed, and hurried down the spiral staircase into the dining room area. As soon as she hit the bottom steps, she could smell the fried potatoes, bacon, and eggs, along with the coffee.

Dwight wasn't up yet, so she sat with Terri at the kitchen table and devoured her breakfast.

After breakfast, she walked outside into the brisk morning air. Shelby tilted her head toward the new morning sky and smiled at the sunbeams as they broke through the clouds and tickled her face with their warmth. It was a wonderful morning. She never imagined that this holiday would turn out to be so pleasant and so full of surprises. To actually see a Black family as successful as Dwight's was as refreshing as the morning air. They seemed to stay under the radar and no one even knew they existed. This family was the equivalent of the 1980's Huxtables in 2010, but the difference was they were the real deal.

She was glad that she'd gotten up early even though she'd been quite tired from the long drive yesterday. Why in the world would I want to sleep when there is so much to enjoy in the environment, she thought. Sleep is a waste of time. I want to take in as much of this as possible. Shelby strolled back up to the porch and into the house.

The family had gathered in the living room, and they were threading strings of popcorn and candy to add to the already decorated Christmas tree. Dwight's Uncle Major was stringing additional lights around the tree, while his aunt Beverly passed out cups of hot chocolate. The kids were buzzing like wasps around a fiery nest, and the rest of the adults were gathered inside of the living room trying to remember old dances.

"Come on Shelby," Sydney said as she entered the room. "We're about to do the Electric Slide."

Shelby shook her head. "I forgot how to do that one," she lied.

Dwight's cousin Lauren beckoned for Shelby to join them. "Girl, you remember the Electric Slide?"

"Honey, stop being shy and get up there and join the fun," Aunt Connie said. "You're practically family."

Again, Shelby shook her head. "I think I'll go back outside and get some more of this Maine fresh air."

"It is really beautiful out there." Connie nodded.

"Here, take my jacket." Aunt Marjorie handed Shelby a large blue, down-filled parka. "It's still a bit cold out there."

"Thank you," Shelby said and then headed back outdoors.

Shelby spotted Dwight outside with his brothers, Brian and Kirby, and the rest of the children, building a snowman.

"When is Uncle Sig coming?" Meghan asked Dwight.

"I think he'll be here today," Dwight answered.

"Is he going to be wearing his red suit?" Cheyenne asked

"Of course," Princess said. She, at six, was the oldest of the children outside. "It's a tradition."

"Is he going to bring the big red bag?" Emily asked

"Yep," Dwight answered.

"Is he going to bring the gifts?" Pria chimed in with the question.

"Yep," Dwight again answered and smiled.

"What about the story?" Amber walked up next to Dwight and took his hand in hers. "Is he going to tell the story?"

"Definitely," Dwight answered. "Uncle Sig tells the story every year."

"Why does he always tell it?" Amy asked.

Dwight stopped working on the snowman. "I don't know. Uncle Sig has always told the story. Ever since I was a little boy."

Paige, Dwight's niece, jumped into his arms and wrapped her arms around his neck. "I want you to tell the story," she said.

"I can't," Dwight said.

Paige's sparkling doe-like eyes glistened as she titled her head. Their hazel color shifted toward a soft green as the sun struck them. "But I want you to tell them," she said.

"Yeah," Pria agreed.

"Yeah," Amber joined in.

"Yeah," Cheyenne added her two cents.

"We'll see," Dwight said. He sat Paige down and turned toward Shelby. "How about a walk?"

Shelby nodded and accepted Dwight's hand as he led her across the lawn and into a wooded area right next to the lake. Shelby wanted to ask Dwight about this Uncle Sig, the stories, and the red suit. If Uncle Sig was going to wear the suit and carry a bag of gifts, why was he going to do it on the 23rd instead of on Christmas morning? And why did the kids know it was him?

Dwight led Shelby to a covered beach swing, which sat next to a large frozen duck pond. Together, they sat and began swinging.

"How do you like it out here?" Dwight asked.

"It's beautiful Dwight and your family is so nice. Thank you for asking me to be your guest."

"No, thank you for coming." Dwight rose from the swing, reached inside his large, green down parka, and pulled out a small black, felt box. He dropped down slowly on one knee and took Shelby's hand into his. "Shell, we've been going together for almost a year now. We're close friends, we know each other really well, and we've shared so much together. I don't have to look any further. I don't want to look any further." He hesitated to clear his throat and get his words just perfect. "I've found everything that I'm looking for, everything that I need in you."

Dwight opened the small black box and held it out for Shelby to look into.

She coughed. It was a rock big enough to choke a horse.

"Shell, grow old with me," Dwight said. "Do me the honor of becoming my wife."

Shelby was breathless, speechless, in shock. First things first, she thought, breathe. That's it, girl, breathe!"

"Dwight, I don't know what to say," she whispered.

"Say yes."

"I care about you tremendously, Dwight, but—"

"But you don't love me," Dwight said as he rose from his knees.

"That's not what I was going to say. I do love you, Dwight."

"But not in a marrying sort of way?"

"Dwight, please let me finish."

He nodded.

"I do love you, but I can't give you an answer right at this moment. This is a big surprise, Dwight, and I'm going to need some time to think."

"I can accept that answer, but I'm putting you on notice, Ms. Shelby Cole. I love you and so you get prepared to be romanced, wined, dined, pampered, loved, cuddled, protected, and flowered from this day forward."

She laughed. She knew that Dwight was serious and was one of the nicest, sweetest men in the world. She often told herself that Dwight would be a real catch, and definitely make some woman really happy, she just didn't know if she was that woman.

Dwight and Shelby made it back to the house and into the living room just as his cousin Sydney had organized the five other members into a contest of "name that tune."

"Come on, you guys have to join in this," she said to the two of them. "You got out of doing the Electric Slide, but you're not going to get away this time." Sydney directed her comments at Shelby.

Shelby and Dwight took seats on the large leather couch and listened as Sydney took them on a trip down memory lane. Shelby was swept away by Billy Paul, Rolls Royce, Teena Marie, Betty Wright, and Luther Vandross. She listened as Marvin Gaye, the Isley Brothers, The Manhattans, and Teddy Pendergrass serenaded her and everyone else in the room. She listened to the strong voices of Natalie Cole, Aretha Franklin, Gladys Knight, and Diana Ross, Earth, Wind, and Fire, the Mighty O'Jays, LTD, The Commodores, and The Isley Brothers swept her away. Smokey Robinson and the Miracles, Tina Turner, The Four Tops and The Stylistics, and James Brown all took her to another time and place. She was lost in the good times, the times of Motown. It lasted until the sun gave way to the moon, and no one noticed the time.

"He's here!" Brittany shouted. "Uncle Sig's car just pulled up."

The kids ran to the door and stared out bursting with anticipation. Shelby clasped her hands together to hide her nervous curiosity. She just knew Uncle Sig was going to come through the door with a bright red Santa suit, screaming, "Ho! Ho! Ho!"

Uncle Sig strolled to the door, stood just at the entrance, and posed, allowing the doorsill to frame him. Shelby's mouth fell open in shock.

Uncle Sigmund Cheikh wore a tailor-made double-breasted, crimson red, designer suit with a white ascot button-down shirt, and a crimson red, silk tie. At the end of his cuffed red trousers, Shelby saw a pair of crimson red alligator skin shoes by Mauri. On his head, he sported a crimson red fedora, tilted just to the right. His smile looked as though it could light up Manhattan.

Dwight leaned over and whispered into Shelby's ear, "Uncle Sig's suits are legendary. They are like a quirky family tradition. Don't worry, we're not crazy."

Suddenly, everyone inside the house burst into applause. They whistled, clapped, and laughed as Uncle Sig posed and bowed over and over again.

Shelby laughed and clapped enthusiastically. Every family had their own quirky little tradition, she told herself. This one was fun. She was really enjoying herself.

The children surrounded Uncle Sig and led him into the living room to his special seat near the fireplace. He smiled and placed his bright red bag next to him then motioned for Dwight to come over.

"What's up, Uncle Sig?" Dwight asked.

Uncle Sig made a slashing motion across his throat. "I'm hoarse and I've lost my voice," he whispered in a croaking, rasping voice. "You're going to have to tell the story."

Dwight's eyes flew open wide in disbelief. "Me? Uncle Sig, I can't tell—"

Uncle Sig's raised eyebrows cut off Dwight's protests as he handed the bag over to Dwight.

Shelby moved in closer to Dwight wondering what the big deal was, and why Uncle Sig couldn't pass out these gifts even with a sore throat.

Dwight opened the red canvas bag and began to remove large bundled albums and bundled papers. Shelby remained at a loss, despite the fact that everyone's enthusiasm remained high, even the children.

When Dwight unrolled one of the large scroll-like pieces of paper, she understood. It was the Cheikh family tree.

"Okay," Dwight said in a slightly high-pitched and broken voice. "We're going to play the game first, and then I'll tell the story."

The adults moved slowly to the rear of the huddled group and allowed the children to gather upfront. They formed a semi-circle around Dwight.

"Who was Grand Dora's mom?" Dwight asked.

"Mamma Jewel," Emily answered.

"Right, two points for Emily," Dwight said. "And who were Mamma Jewel's mamma and daddy?" he asked.

"Mamma Sweet and Grandpa Timmy," Meghan shouted.

"Good!" Dwight said. "Four points for Meghan. Now, who were Grandpa Timmy's mamma and daddy?"

"Mommy Eddie Mae and Grandpa Louis," Princess answered.

Shelby was suddenly short of breath. She had to get out of the room and out of the house; she needed air. She raced onto the front porch and sat down on the swinging porch bench. Shelby understood now. It all came together; it all made sense. She had expected toys, clothes, and other types of gifts. But what Uncle Sig had brought was more precious than all of the toys and the clothes in the world. He had brought with him a real gift, the gift of family, of history, of roots.

Shelby fumbled with her hands before interlacing her fingers and rocking back and forth in the swing. She had wondered how this family was able to turn out generation after generation of successful, educated, well-rounded individuals, and now she knew. They gave each new generation a foundation to stand on, a legacy to uphold, roots to nourish, and a supporting, nurturing, loving environment in which to flourish.

She could hear Dwight through the living room window. He told the story of his family's history, recounting each generation and their struggles and their accomplishments, all to the claps and cheers of the children. This man, the man she thought had no depth, no history, no rhythm, no soul, was now recounting the history of a family whose service, dedication, and sacrifice to their people dated back hundreds of years.

Shelby buried her head into her hands and began to weep. She had been so wrong, so silly, and so shallow. Her tears flowed steadily for several moments before she felt a tap on her shoulder. Startled, she raised her head quickly to find Uncle Sig standing before her with his gigantic smile.

"What's the matter, young lady?" he asked.

Shelby quickly wiped away the tears streaming down her cheeks. "Oh, it's nothing," she said. She glanced back over her shoulder and peered through the blinds of the living room window.

"Your family, it's just so…so beautiful."

Uncle Sig smiled and waved his hand toward the bench. "May I sit with you?" he asked.

Shelby nodded yes.

Uncle Sig sat down next to her and produced a soft, white silk handkerchief. He handed her the handkerchief and then wrapped his arm around her.

"Everything is alright, young lady. You just cheer yourself up. It's Christmas."

"I know, I know," Shelby said. "I was just sitting here thinking, and, well, my emotions got the best of me. Hey, wait a minute… your voice!"

Uncle Sig smiled and lowered his head. Shelby looked at his puffy cheeks and noticed the twinkle in his deep brown eyes. She knew he was embarrassed.

"I'm not getting any younger," Uncle Sig said. "It was time to pass on the story-telling to the next generation."

"So, you pretended that your throat was sore!"

"That's the way it was passed on to me," Uncle Sig said with a smile. "If it wouldn't have been for my uncle Lamar's sore throat I would have never taken over when I did."

"And a whole generation would have missed out on those fabulous red suits!" Shelby said.

They laughed together.

"Wait a minute, is Dwight going to have to wear those things?" she asked.

Uncle Sig laughed again. "No. Every generation adds their own flair and has their own style of presentation. My uncle Lamar's suits were green." Uncle Sig leaned over and nudged Shelby's shoulder with his own. "Can you imagine me wearing a green suit?"

Again, they laughed.

The big white door creaked open and Dwight stepped out. "What's up guys?" he asked.

Uncle Sig grabbed his throat and whispered in a raspy voice, "Just getting some advice on this old throat of mine." Having finished, Uncle Sig got up and headed back into the house.

Dwight sat down on the bench next to Shelby and smiled at her. "What's up Shell?" he asked.

Shelby turned her body on the bench facing him. She took his hand into hers. "Dwight you have a wonderful family. And, well…they remind me a little bit of my own. They are always there for you, always willing to help out, and give advice. I remember one piece of advice my mother gave me when I was younger. She told me to never be afraid to admit when you're wrong. You'll lose friends and sleep if you do."

She released Dwight's hand and crossed her arms as the chill of the evening air struck her. "My mother used to give me a lot of advice," she continued. "We used to talk about relationships, and about finding true love. I always pictured my Knight in Shining Armor, my Romeo, and my Prince Charming, coming and sweeping me off my feet, and carrying me off into the sunset. I never thought my Romeo would sneak up on me, or that he would be so comfortable, so easy to talk to. I didn't know that he would start off being my dear, sweet, kind friend."

Shelby threw her head back in laughter, and raked her hand through her hair, sending it over her shoulders. "I was told that love blindsides you, not creeps up on you, and wraps itself around you like a warm, comfortable old blanket on a cold winter's afternoon. And that's why I didn't know, that's why I didn't recognize it. I didn't see it. I was looking in all the wrong places, for all of the wrong signs."

She took Dwight's hand into hers again. "I, Shelby Denise Cole, love you, Dwight Antoine Cheikh. And I would consider myself the luckiest woman on earth if you would have me as your wife."

Dwight pulled the small, felt box from his pocket, opened it, and removed the ring. He placed it on her finger.

Shelby giggled the whole time he was placing the ring on her finger. She felt dizzy, like she was floating.

"Did my uncle have anything to do with this?" Dwight asked suspiciously.

Shelby laughed. "No, silly. Your uncle and I were discussing something else."

"Him pretending to have a sore throat so that he could pass the story-telling on to me?" Dwight raised an eyebrow.

"Dwight!" Shelby said, surprised. "Now what makes you think that?" They hugged, got up, and went back into the house to share their good news with the family.

That night Shelby lay in the bed and thought about the day's events. How odd, two days before Christmas, and gifts were passed out like there was no tomorrow. She had a fiancée who was going to make a wonderful husband. Dwight was given the honor of being the guardian of his family's treasured history, the librarian of all that is sacred to them and makes them who they are. The children received the best gift of all. They were given a foundation of dignity, a legacy of accomplishment, and an abundance of family love to stand on. Shelby knew that it was a precious gift that they would be given every year until they went off to Fisk, Howard, Spelman, and Morehouse to become doctors, lawyers, and scientists. Judging from their enthusiasm, they understood what a precious gift they were being given, as well.

After Dwight had proposed to her earlier that afternoon, they went back inside and she was officially welcomed into the family. The warm hugs, the kisses, and the advice from the older women who had married into the family would be invaluable. She also smiled as she thought about the celebration they had after the announcement. Dwight's family loved to have a good time. They cranked up the CD player and danced down memory lane for the rest of the evening. They did the Electric Slide again, and the Wop, the Calypso, the Jerk, the Penguin, the Camel Walk, the Flirt, and every other dance they could think of. Dwight even joined in and did his little rhythm-less herky-jerky. Eventually, even Granny-Gran danced a little.

Shelby rolled on her side and laughed heartily as she visualized Granny-Gran's dancing. She performed the most elegant rendition of the Butterfly and the Tootsie Roll Shelby had ever seen.

In Perpetuity

Frederick Williams

Young Marshall Taylor stared up at the clock on the wall. It was a little after 6:00 p.m. and he had to be home before seven. He had been in the Carver Library for over two hours and in that time had completed all his homework except for his geometry assignment due the next day in his third-period class. Later on that evening, he'd go over to Tanika's apartment and get the assignment from her. She was a whiz in math and always helped him. He knew she really liked him and so he played on that fact to get what he needed from her. And that was always the homework assignment for geometry. He hadn't hit that yet, but would probably have to sometime in the near future just to keep her doing those things he needed from her. The problem was that she had nothing to attract him physically. She was Black with nappy hair and extremely big lips, nose, and just not attractive. But then again, ugly girls needed loving, too.

Marshall closed his history book and packed it and the other books he'd spread out on the table into his book bag. He had an hour to kill before he'd have to get home. Going to the Carver Library after school was not his favorite thing to do. He'd rather hang out with his niggahs and his dawgs. But Mamma insisted that he spend time in the library instead of on the street. The only good part about being in the library was that he could get on one of the computers. With no computer at home, he liked to spend at least a half-hour on one at the library. His mother had promised that sometime soon she'd buy him and his younger sister Angela a computer. Marshall knew that probably wouldn't happen anytime soon. They survived on the very little money his father James gave them whenever they could catch up with him and the money Phyllis earned working the counter at the local McDonald's on Walter Street. They struggled to make it from week to week with the basic necessities and there was no way Phyllis could find money to buy a computer.

Marshall got up and sauntered over to the computer room filled with others like him who needed to get on the Internet and also retrieve e-mails. He found one empty spot, sat down, and turned it on. He searched "My Space" until he found the one person he communicated with at that same time every day.

"Hey, Dawg, wuzzup?" The message read.

"Usual, being hassled by my mama for doing what comes natural," Marshall replied and waited for another message.

"Yeah, I know, these old people can't get right with us 'cause they don't want to let us be us."

"I know that's right. I'm still tripping about last Sunday at church and then when I got home."

"Oh yeah, what's that all about?"

"It was a real B-day for me. Let me run it down to ya. Here goes."

That particular Sunday the church had been packed. Marshall, Phyllis, and Angela found seats in the back pew. They usually sat up front, but this day they were late arriving and were fortunate to find enough room to sit together. Marshall entered the row first and made his way until he was right next to a young, pretty Black girl, who sat there with a child. Marshall sat down and left a little room between him and the girl. He noticed the disdainful glare Phyllis shot at the young lady. She grabbed Marshall by the shoulder and forced him to slide toward her. She then moved past him and took the seat next to the young lady.

After church, Marshall worked up enough nerve and asked his mother, "Mamma, why did you make me move in church?"

"Because I don't want you sittin' next to no sinner," Phyllis scowled. "That girl, the one that had that baby and ain't married. I ain't gon' have you gettin' caught up in no mess like that." Phyllis turned and glared at her son.

"Yes, ma'am," Marshall whispered. He didn't really understand his mother. She had never married his father so she was also looking down on them as a family. It made no sense because just about everyone who lived in their apartment complex was single. There were no fathers and it was just like the families where he lived existed of only a mother and the children. Why be so hard on that young girl when she was doing just like all the other young girls? Whenever he did decide to get with Tanika, he'd have to be careful; he sure didn't want to get her pregnant.

Marshall hustled up the steps to their apartment, leaving his sister and mother behind. He unlocked the door, hurried to his room, and changed clothes. He hit the ON button on the radio and instantly the room filled with the words from the rapper, Too Short. Immediately, a barrage of "niggahs," "bitches," and "dawgs" poured out of the radio.

He heard his mother walking outside the room and knew what was coming.

"Marshall, turn that junk off," she shrieked. "How dare you just come from church and start playing all that profanity?"

"But, Mama, it's our music, just like you all had your music in the past," Marshall said as he complied with his mother and turned the radio off. He got up and walked out of the room.

"Why you so hard on us 'cause we got our choice in music? I bet Grandma was just as hard on you with your music."

"Don't matter, our music wasn't filled with all that filth," Phyllis said as she walked into the kitchen and started to put dishes up in the cabinet. "You're not going to insult Black women by listening to that junk in my house. And that's just my rules. When you grow up you can do what you want in your own place."

"Mama, they're just words," Marshall said making his last appeal and knowing it would do no good. "You old people need to get up with the times. It's just words," Marshall finished and went back into his bedroom.

****

"Say, young brotha, how long you going to use this computer?" asked a man standing directly behind Marshall.

Marshall jerked and looked at the man. "Just a little longer," he answered. "I got a friend on Facebook who I talk with every day right about this time."

"I was wondering 'cause there are a few things I'd like to show you."

Marshall studied the man in some detail. He'd never seen him in the library before. And he dressed differently than what most folks did in his neighborhood. He appeared to be from another time in history. Most of the brothers in Marshall's neighborhood would crack up laughing if this man walked down his street. He was tempted to ask the man where he came from, but had learned long ago not to delve into other people's business. His mother always told him what he didn't know he shouldn't know.

"Say, little brotha why you looking at me so hard, something you want to ask me?"

"No sir," Marshall said as he turned back and signed off the computer. Suddenly he swung back around. "Yeah," he said to the man. "Why you dressed like that and where you from?"

"It's the way we dressed during my time and I'm from the same Black community that you live in."

Marshall leaned away from the man and looked for Mary the librarian. This man was acting weird and he wanted to make sure other people were still in the library even though he knew they were.

"What you talking about man? I ain't ever seen you in my neighborhood."

"I visit your classroom on occasion and know your instructor teaches you better than to say ain't." The man moved in closer to Marshall who jumped up and moved further away.

"Marshall, are you all right?" Mary asked as she walked toward him. "And who are you talking to?"

Marshall jerked his head to the right and glared at the man, and then looked at Mary. "What do you mean, who am I—"

"Stop," the man interrupted. "I'm afraid you may appear to be silly to the lady."

Marshall turned away from Mary and again concentrated on this strange man who obviously he could see, but no one else could.

"Marshall Taylor, who are you talking to, and what is wrong with you?" Mary again asked him.

"If you tell her that a man is standing over here next to you, she's going to think you're on drugs and are hallucinating," the man warned Marshall before he could respond to Mary.

The young boy sat back down and looked straight ahead. Now he was more curious than he was afraid. There wasn't much this strange person could do in the library and why would he want to harm him.

"Who are you?" Marshall whispered and quickly glanced over at Mary to make sure she didn't hear him.

"I am In Perpetuity," the man answered as he put his large, strong hand on Marshall's shoulder.

"You're what?" Marshall shrieked and quickly put his hand over his mouth as he looked in Mary's direction. She didn't look up.

"In Perpetuity means always. It might be a stretch but I use it for emphasis with young Black men like you."

Marshall no longer feared this strange man, but instead wanted to know more about him. He glared at the clock. He needed to be home by six to start dinner and see about his sister. Phyllis would be home by seven; he had to get there before she did, but he couldn't let this man get away. He felt a strong attraction to him.

"You trying to tell me that you been on Earth forever?" Marshall quipped and again shot a glance over at Mary.

"I'm not telling you that at all. You know the physical body cannot last forever. That was not the purpose the Lord had for the body. What I am telling you is that I carry with me the essence of our culture." The man stopped for a moment and took in a deep breath. "It is ideas of who and what we are passed on through the generations. It defines the meaning of a group of people who have coalesced in a survival mode. It is also agreed upon behavior patterns, speech, music, dance, and most importantly how they treat each other. It is respect for all the individuals in the group."

"How do you define yourself?" Marshall didn't know where that question came from. It's not something he would ask in a normal conversation. This man had affected him to reach deep in the depths of his own thinking he never knew he possessed.

"Good question." The man smiled. "I am already having an influence on you. No doubt you'll be an excellent student after our discussion. I define myself on the behavior of all our people. I am a composite of all our people from the inception of our existence here in this country until this day, right now, right here with you. I am the collective body of all the years and vast experiences both pleasant and unpleasant of Black people. Unfortunately, most of our experiences in this country have been unpleasant and that is part of the reason why we treat each other the way that we do."

"Why do you say that most of our experience here has been unpleasant?" Marshall asked. "I've had a pretty good life, even though we are poor."

"You are a part of a collective body," the man said. "The Black experience in America did not begin with you, you are only an extension or continuation. You are only fifteen and your collective experience goes back to the first time back in 1619 when the first African landed on the shores of this country and had his past wiped out. He had no past, but only a present and future."

"That sounds real confusing to me," Marshall whispered as a young girl walked past him.

"Let me explain it to you in this fashion. We arrived in this country in 1619 and from the middle of that century until 1865 we were forced to be slaves against our will. From 1865 until right to this day in 2011 we have been out of slavery but forced to exist under a horrendous system of apartheid until about 1964 when Dr. Martin Luther King, Jr. helped end segregation. So, let's calculate, from 1650 to 1865 is two hundred and fifteen years, and from 1865 until 1964 is another ninety-nine years. Let's see, that adds up to three hundred and four years, as opposed to forty-six years of real freedom. With those kinds of numbers no wonder we struggle with our own identity. We have a lot of years of oppression to overcome and we're just getting started. I have a great deal of work in front of me."

Marshall again perked up and wanted to shout out his next question but he was very much aware of Mary sitting at the desk. He toned it down and asked, "Is that why we talk so harshly and ugly about each other?"

"Exactly! It reflects all the negative experiences we encountered in a country that oppressed us and has never liked us as a people."

"You should've been in church with us a few Sundays ago when my mother—"

"I was there," the man interrupted.

"How do you feel about the way my mother referred to that young girl sitting in our pew?"

"She is simply a reflection of what has happened to us for those first three hundred and four years."

"I need a better answer than that." Marshall felt he could get aggressive in his discussion with this man who claimed to be the collective experience of Black people in America. "Culture is supposed to be something good. You can't tell me the way she acted and the words she used was a positive thing."

"You really are getting pretty deep into this young man. I'm impressed."

"Mister, I don't mean to be rude, but I don't have much time. I got to get home, look after my sister, and on top of that get supper started before my mother gets there. If you can answer my question it would sure help me out a lot. I want to understand how my Mamma can look at another woman in that light?"

The man took in a deep breath and slowly released it. "You have centuries of a race insecure within themselves but powerful people with all kinds of weapons of destruction, tearing down your ancestors in order to build themselves up. Blacks have been forced to succumb to a distorted view as projected by these insecure people. After a while, we began to believe their lies."

"Why do white people hate us so much?" Marshall asked. "If you really look at what happened, we should be the ones full of hate, but instead we want to be like them, you know, dress like them, talk like them, and most of all look like them."

"You're way ahead of your time," the man said. "That kind of thinking and understanding should only come to you much later in life. But since you are already at that point, let me show you the truth."

The man gestured for Marshall to get up. He then sat down and punched some codes into the computer. When the site popped up on the screen, he got up and let Marshall sit back down. "Watch, listen, and learn."

The site illuminated a scene from sometime in the past. Five men wearing long white wigs and dressed in colonial garb, sat at a large table reading some kind of document. Marshall turned up the volume just loud enough for him to hear what they were saying, but not disturb the other people using the computers next to him. He listened intently.

"What is this, Thomas?" one of the men asked.

"It is the results of my experiment I carried out on my slaves," Thomas Jefferson answered. "I needed to find out if Africans, who are our slaves, are really human beings just like us, or are they closer to the animal kingdom." Jefferson paused and allowed the magnitude of his comment to sink in with the others. "If they are human beings created by God in the same manner that He created us then based on what I wrote in the Declaration of Independence and what we claim in the new Constitution, we cannot keep them as slaves. We cannot have men and women equal to us as our slaves. It is against the laws of human nature and God."

The other men stirred around in their chairs and looked with much more intensity at the document.

"What are you saying and doing, Thomas?" one of the men spoke up. "We can't afford to prove that the African is our equal. It'll be the ruin of us all. We need our slaves to maintain our standard of living and our lifestyle."

"John's right, Thomas," another man said. "And furthermore, who'll do our work in the fields?"

"Yeah, and who'll do all the work in the kitchen for my wife?" the fourth man added. "She'll divorce me if she has to lift a pot and sweep a floor."

All the others laughed.

"Don't worry men," Jefferson said reassuring them. "My findings vindicate us and actually prove that we are doing these poor beasts a favor." He stopped, picked up the document, and turned to a certain page. "Look at my findings on page 15. I have proof that these poor creatures are by nature lazy, slow thinking, over-sexed, and easily frightened."

The men grunted in unison. They smiled their approval.

"As you may have noticed, if you get too close to one of them," Jefferson continued. "They have the most vile body odor."

"You're being nice, Thomas," the fourth man said. "They just plain old stink."

"And there is a reason," again Jefferson spoke up. "Unlike normal human beings like us, they have trouble passing material out of their bodies."

"They just can't take a good crap," one of the men said.

Marshall suddenly jerked back, turned, and stared at the man.

"I know, it's hard to stomach," he said. "Every time I reveal this to a new neophyte like you, I get angry. But anger won't change our condition; knowledge will. And knowledge is nothing more than knowing and learning. So, turn back and learn."

Marshall followed the stranger's instructions. He knew he should be home by now, but he had to know more, even at the risk of a whipping when he got there. He turned his attention back to the men, anxious to know how much more damage one of the country's greatest leaders, one he was taught to admire and respect, had really done to the image of his people.

"Since they have trouble passing material out of their bodies," Jefferson continued. "It backs up in their system and comes out in their pores. That means they are not fully developed as human beings. If placed on God's scale of human development, they would fall lower than man, but just above animals. In fact, it is the truth that an African woman would be just as content and happy being married to an ape."

Again, all the men in the room got a good laugh.

"So, my friends, when I said all men are created equal, I was referring to all human beings. God made human beings equal, and since my study has proven that Africans are not fully developed human beings, but a cross between humans and animals, we do not have to look upon them as equals."

Smiles spread across the collective faces of the other men. One of them spoke for the rest.

"Then that means we are not going against the word of God or against our beloved Declaration of Independence and Constitution if we don't treat these people as equals."

"Correction my friend," Jefferson interjected. "Not people, but subhumans."

The men again burst out laughing and the image before Marshall faded away.

He sat there and stared at the screen. "Did they really believe that?" he asked the strange man.

"It doesn't matter whether they believed it or not," the man said as he leaned over Marshall's shoulder and pulled up another site. "What matters is that they acted on their misguided beliefs and as a result, millions of our people suffered." He pointed at the screen as another picture appeared. "Look, listen, and learn," the man instructed.

Marshall stared with anger and trepidation as the scene developed before him.

Twenty-five to thirty haggardly looking white men stood in front of a large platform lifted a few inches off the ground. To their right were at least ten Blacks; five men, three women, and two children about five years of age. Four guards with shotguns held high stood at each end of the Blacks, intently staring at them.

A neatly dressed white man entered the yard and hurried to the front of the group of white men. He smiled at one of the men in the front of the line.

"Hey, Sam, I see you right up front. Guess you want a close-up view of these niggers, especially the wenches." He laughed. "Guess you probably going to buy the wench with the biggest backside."

The other man broke out in a loud laugh. "Gotta get mine," he said. "But I've got to buy two good size bucks and one of them bitches for a client down in Natchez. I should make a pretty good profit. He was desperate to get some niggers to work his fields. Seems that they had some kind of epidemic down there. Killed off a bunch of their niggers and they got to replace them right away. Can't get behind on working the fields. Too much money involved.

"I'll see if I can help you out, make sure you get the best of the bunch. Then maybe you'll give me a little something extra," the auctioneer said as he signaled for the guard to bring the first slave to be sold that day.

The first slave, a young naked woman who appeared to be about sixteen was forced up on the platform by one of the guards.

Marshall turned away when he saw the naked girl, but the strange man grabbed him by the shoulders and forced him to look back at the screen.

"Look and learn," he said.

Marshall glared at the man, but knew what he was doing for him would be beneficial in his understanding of what really happened to his people and the brutality of it all. He turned his attention back to the screen.

He couldn't help but notice the sorrow written all over the young girl's face as she lowered her head down looking at the ground instead of what was happening all around her. It struck him as interesting that many of the young girls in his school and neighborhood often walked with their heads down and backs slumped just like this young girl. The girls in his neighborhood needed to see this young girl who was also Black but lived over one hundred fifty years ago. Too bad she couldn't come back to this world today and let some of her sisters in the future see how much better they had it than she did in such a vicious and oppressive system. Bingo! It dawned on Marshall that is exactly what the strange man had done. No wonder he forced him to look back at the screen. What Marshall didn't understand is why he had been picked to have so much of his people's past revealed to him?

"Git your head up, bitch, before I lay this whip to your back," the auctioneer shouted. "Act like you happy that these fine men would consider even buying your lazy behind."

The young girl held her head up but still looked away into the distance, just as if she was dreaming of a place across the ocean.

"Come on boys, let's start the bidding on this fine, young and healthy wench. She a good worker and she got a whole lot of child-rearing years ahead of her." None of the men immediately responded. The auctioneer continued. "Come on men, get in closer to this bitch. Feel on her strong and healthy breasts, her firm backside and she got all her teeth."

The auctioneer now looked up at the girl. "Open your mouth so these men can see how healthy your teeth is." The young girl complied with the man's instructions.

Five of the men, including the man the auctioneer, was talking with before the bidding opened, moved in much closer and surrounded the girl.

"Bend over," one of the men instructed her.

She did.

Another of the men felt on her legs and another squeezed her breasts. Finally, another man popped her on the backside. They all laughed.

"You see how that meat just bounce like jelly?"

Again, all the men laughed then moved back to their original positions so the bidding could begin. The man the auctioneer had talked with started the bidding.

"Three hundred dollars," he shouted.

"I'll go six hundred," a man from the back, who hadn't come up front to examine the girl, shouted.

"How you going to bid from way back there," the first man said. "I'll go seven hundred and no higher. Anyone wants to go higher than that, then you can have the bitch."

"Seven hundred and fifty," the man who had slapped the young girl on her backside said. "It's worth that to have her around just to be able to slap that rear end."

"Okay, seven hundred and fifty, going, going, gone," the auctioneer cut the bidding off. No further discussion was necessary. It was no one's business how he planned to use the young girl. All that mattered was that he got a good price for her, which meant a nice profit for the owner, which would result in a nice bonus for the auctioneer.

The scene slowly faded out and Marshall, now angry, turned to face the strange man.

"Why are you showing me this?" he asked. "It's really making me mad. Makes me want to go out there and kick some white butt."

"Remember young man, not anger but knowledge," the man instructed. "When you get angry, they win. When you get knowledge, you win."

"I think I'm beginning to understand why we treat each other the way we do," Marshall said. "Is there any more I need to see in order to understand much better?"

"Take this final trip with me," the stranger said and hit the proper keys on the keyboard to bring up another scene.

Marshall was already late, his mother would fuss and probably whip him, but it would all be worth it for the knowledge. He turned and faced the screen and anticipated the next scene.

Three figures, a woman and two children, ran along the banks of the river. Snow-covered the ground and a strong wind blew in their face. It slowed them down, but they appeared determined and would not be stopped. She saw the house on top of the hill and the lantern in the window. She had to get there before the men chasing from behind caught up with her and returned her back across the river into Kentucky.

Marshall turned and stared at the man as if to question why the woman and two children were running. But the man held his hand up as a signal to just look and learn. He turned his attention back to the scene before him.

Snow blurred the woman's image but she seemed to know the house on the hill would protect them. The woman looked behind her but could not see much. She did know, however, that the pursuers weren't far behind them.

"Mamma, I'm cold and I can't run anymore," the younger of the two children, a girl about seven, said.

"No, baby, you can't stop," the mother pleaded. "We have to keep moving. We can't go back. We just can't go back." She grabbed the girl's hand and jerked her forward. She held her other hand out, and the boy, who was a little older, took it.

Marshall again turned his attention away from the scene developing before him. He compared what he was watching with his family, a mother with two children, the oldest a boy, and the youngest, a girl. They were frightened and were desperately trying to find their way to safety. He had to find out how this would turn out.

"I'm okay, Mamma," the boy said. "All we have to do is make it to that house and we'll be safe?" he asked.

"Yes, baby, that's all we have to do," she answered then looked behind her. She knew it would happen. Images of men on horseback were visible. She looked straight ahead and the house on the hill was still some distance from them. The woman looked in all directions for a place to possibly hide, but nothing was there.

The young girl's legs went out from under her and the mother had to drag her along. She finally lifted her into her arms and that slowed them down considerably. The snow was getting heavier and the wind had picked up. No doubt the wind chill had to be close to zero. The young girl began to cry. Finally, they fell down in the snow knowing that soon the slave hunters would be on them and their desperate attempt to escape their personal hell would be over. No doubt they would be returned to Kentucky and the children would be sold or traded to one of the Deep South plantations. The woman hugged her two children tightly and prayed that God would take them out of this misery.

She could now hear the barking dogs that would lead the men right to them. She held her children tightly and cried.

Marshall took his open hand and hit the computer, practically knocking it off the stand. He stared at the strange man who had a solemn expression.

"Did that kind of thing really happen or is this some kind of mean game you're playing on me?" he asked.

"It happened all the time under the laws of what was called the Fugitive Slave Law of 1850. Any white man could capture a Black person, didn't matter if they were a slave or not, and take them back into the South and slavery."

"Why did our government let that kind of thing happen?"

"Because they looked at our ancestors as niggers and bitches. Called them those names no different than that music you think is so cool and, as you told your mother, just words, nothing more. They made jokes about our physical features and the color of our skin and used it as a reason to do what you just saw. They used our beautiful Black women in the same manner that you have used Tanika."

"How do you know about Tanika?"

"Because I am culture perpetuity and a hundred years from now, I will let some young Black men know how you treated a beautiful Black sister, Tanika, in the same manner that those animals treated our women back then."

"No, you can't—"

"Yes, I can, and, yes, I will. In fact, I'll be obligated to do just that. I will tell the future generations that you used Tanika because you saw her as being ugly and your concept of beauty is copied after the very people who have oppressed us for hundreds of years. Do you know that we are the only race of people who want to look like the people who committed some of the most atrocious crimes in history against our people, against Black women who looked like Tanika, and because they didn't meet a certain standard of beauty, it was all right, just like it's all right for you to disrespect that young lady." The stranger reached over Marshall and hit the play button creating another scene on the computer screen.

"Watch this last scene, brace yourself for what you are about to see, and wake up young man."

"I don't think I want to," Marshall said and tried to turn away from the computer. "I should have been home a half-hour ago."

The stranger placed his large hand on Marshall's shoulder preventing him from getting up.

"You're all right," he said. "Your mother is okay with you being late because she knows you are caught up in a knowledge blast. After we finish, she also knows that you will be converted from the ignorance of your history and culture to the light.

Marshall sighed then reluctantly turned and stared at the computer.

A very dark-skinned young woman stood handcuffed and surrounded by a group of white men. They appeared to be drunk. The leader of the men moved closer to a tree with a long-extended branch about ten feet off the ground.

"This one will do," he said to a man holding a rope. "Throw it over the top of this branch and tighten it up."

The man moved under the tree branch and tossed the rope over the top. He tightened it with the end of the rope in a noose.

"That's it, sheriff. It's ready to do the job," the man said.

"Okay, boys, throw that old bitch up top of the horse, and let's get that rope around her Black nigger neck. Sass me, will you?" he said as he glared at the woman who just stared at the ground.

Two men grabbed the young girl and threw her on top of the horse. They then placed the noose around her neck.

One of the men laughed and said, "Hey, sheriff, we ain't killin' jest one nigger. This bitch is pregnant. We gon' git rid of two of them. Two for one, and the world is a better place."

The men laughed.

Marshall turned his head away from the scene. He didn't want to see what was about to happen.

"Okay, mister, I've seen enough. I get your point, now I'm going home."

The stranger again placed his hand on Marshall's shoulder and that locked him in place. Sternly, he said, "Look and learn. Learning is knowledge. You young boys don't know, and it is our fault. If you knew, you wouldn't dare use the same terms and misuse our Black women the way you do. That terminology led to tremendous suffering for your ancestors."

Marshall couldn't do anything but sit and stare at the monitor. He grimaced as one of the men slapped the horse. It sprinted forward and the woman dangled from the branch. Her body began to convulse.

One of the men smiled and took a drink from a bottle. He then snatched a long Bowie knife out of his belt and strutted up to the woman.

"Y'all watch what I'm goin' do." He took his knife back and then swung it forward. It came down and across the front of the woman's stomach. Blood shot everywhere and the fully developed baby fell to the ground.

"What have you done?" one of the men shouted.

"Kill the little nigger. Stomp on it," another man shouted.

The man smiled, lifted his big boot, and brought it crashing down on the baby's head.

"NO!" Marshall shouted.

"Young man, what in the world is wrong with you?" Mary asked from behind her desk.

Marshall buried his head between his hands and sobbed.

The librarian got up and rushed over to him. "Why are you crying? What's wrong?"

He pointed to the screen without saying a word.

Mary stared at the blank monitor. "Are you all right? There's nothing on this monitor."

Marshall looked up at a blank monitor. He turned to his left and the stranger was gone. He then glared at Mary.

"I'm okay," he said.

"Why were you shouting?" she asked. "You know that kind of behavior is not allowed in here. Please don't do it again." She turned and walked back to her desk.

Marshall stared at the blank monitor. He wanted that old and funny-dressed Black man to come back. He was due an explanation for what he had to endure from all four of those visuals. Marshall smiled as he thought it all had been some kind of a joke. Because if what he'd just witnessed really did happen and the words nigger and bitch helped facilitate that kind of cruelty, he would swear off, not only those two words but all music that used them. He needed some kind of sign, something left behind as proof. Without some kind of verification, he would assume that this had been nothing more than his imagination at work overtime.

Now he had to rush home and take his punishment. But the stranger said that his mother knew why he was late and would not be upset. If when he arrived home, she did not fuss at him that would be proof of the stranger's existence in the library and proof that what he saw was the truth.

Marshall ran up the two flights of stairs, unlocked the door, and rushed inside the apartment. He braced for the explosion as he walked into the kitchen area where Phyllis was preparing dinner.

"Mamma, don't go off. I met some crazy guy who showed me all these ugly things that happened to Black people in the past."

"I know," Phyllis said without looking up.

"You ain't mad at me, Mamma? You ain't going to whip me?"

"Not at all," Phyllis answered. "Now go get ready for dinner."

A shocked Marshall hurried to his bedroom. This was all getting too crazy. What he experienced at the library couldn't have really happened. It was too cruel and ugly. And it would make him feel bad for all the times he'd enjoyed the music that used words that brought extreme pain and suffering to his ancestors. His music meant too much to him. He needed more evidence in order to believe what happened. He needed physical proof. Marshall would become a convert if the stranger came back and gave him something more to hang on to.

He hesitated before he went into the bedroom. Marshall let out a big sigh and opened the door. After turning on the light he froze in place. There on the bed was a small trinket with the inscription "IN PERPETUITY."

Losing the Game

Michael Smith

Malik Williams sped his Mustang into the parking lot outside the downtown Metropolitan Police Department. He shot a glance at the clock on the dashboard in his car. It read 3:58, and roll call for the afternoon shift would start at 4:00 p.m. He knew Platoon Sergeant Dennis Washburn would commence to call roll right on the hour. The man was like clockwork. He never deviated from his procedure. And he never deviated from the hard, cold stare he gave any officer who was late. Sergeant considered any arrival after the second hand had passed the number twelve, indicating it was four o'clock as late. That's why Malik was pushing hard to find a parking space and get inside. He finally found one, pulled into the space, jumped out of his car, and ran into the building. It was now 3:59, and he had one minute to spare.

Today was especially important because Sergeant Washburn would make the monthly announcement of new assignments. Malik had put in a request to be transferred to the Community Service Unit. As he ran through the long corridor and finally burst into the roll call room, he knew his chance of getting that transfer was slim to none. He had been a beat cop for only three years and hadn't paid his dues for such a plush transfer. But he had to try, simply because of his promise he had made to himself when he first joined the force. At some point in his career, he wanted to help save young Black kids instead of throwing them in jail to waste away and become yet another statistic of a lost young man or woman, who under different circumstances might have become a doctor, lawyer, or scientist. Instead of arresting them, he wanted to save them. And that's why the afternoon's roll call was so important to him.

"Welcome, Malik" Sergeant Washburn called out. "I'm glad you could make it just seconds before roll call."

Malik found a seat in the very back of the room. "You got it, Sarge," he said. "As long as it's a few seconds before the hour and not after, I'm okay."

"I can't argue with that," Sergeant Washburn replied. "But that's got to be awfully hard on your nerves knowing you were so close to getting the stare."

Malik relaxed back in his chair and smiled. "You right about that. Nobody in this room wants to get that stare."

"All right, men and ladies, today we announce the new promotions and transfers," Sergeant Washburn said, abruptly changing the subject and getting to the business for the afternoon.

Malik sat quietly, praying, and holding his breath as if those acts would deliver the new assignment he wanted to him. Dead silence engulfed the room and you could hear a pin drop. There were over a hundred officers in that room and way over half were hoping to hear their name called.

"Okay, listen up," Sergeant Washburn's voice increased a couple of decibels. "The officers who have been transferred to..."

He stopped and stared, with a frown on his face, at the paper in front of him.

Sergeant Washburn knew exactly what he was doing, Malik thought. He's just messing with us. He deliberately stopped in order to make us suffer just a little bit longer. But Malik didn't care what silly games he played just as long as his name was called.

"Officers Parker and Hernandez," Sergeant continued, "and Officer Roberts have all been transferred to the Community Services Unit."

"All right, way to go," Officer Parker said. He got up and reached to slap hands with the other two. Dejected, Malik watched as the three men congratulated each other then sat back down.

"Congratulations, gentlemen," Sergeant Washburn now shouted above the chatter coming from all over the room. "The effective date of your new unit assignment will start after completion of your shift today."

Malik's head dropped and his shoulders slumped. The transfer would have meant so much to him, and now he would have to wait another six months before he could even apply again. The razzing from the other officers hadn't started but it was coming. They all knew how badly he wanted that transfer, and the fact that he didn't get it would leave him vulnerable to some serious teasing. The older men on the force had labeled him "bleeding heart" and stayed on his case. They knew he dedicated his spare time visiting the high schools, detention facilities, and going to community events advising children about the dangers of gangs and drugs.

"Hey, Malik, now you can take your mind off saving these bad little juvenile delinquents and concentrate on throwing them behind bars where they belong," one of the officers shouted out loud enough for all to hear. The officers busted out laughing.

"Yeah, if they gave awards for saving souls instead of locking up gangsters, he'd be a sure winner," another officer shouted.

"And then we'd all be looking for jobs," a third man called out. "People like him go around trying to save these hoodlums, and then we won't have nobody to arrest, and that'll put us in the unemployment lines."

Again, the officers laughed. They seemed to be enjoying themselves at Malik's expense.

The laughter and the sounds faded as Malik drifted off into his own world. Growing up right in the inner city, he could relate to the kids they were talking about. Some of the crimes they committed he had actually done himself as a young man and at the time honestly didn't know they were illegal. It made him feel like a hypocrite. How could he possibly take them downtown for things he had done on the same streets of Cleveland, Ohio. Some of the infractions went on so much and often in his neighborhood growing up they had become socially acceptable to the community. But to the other officers who worked those same streets with him but had grown up in a different environment, things that seemed petty, were crimes to them, and the offenders received no understanding or sympathy regardless of age.

Malik took in a deep breath and sighed as he listened to the Sergeant take back control of the room.

"I'm still conducting roll call," he shouted. Sergeant's face turned beet red as he stared down at the second list of names for transfer. "The following men have been promoted to the status of detective and assigned to the Criminal Investigation Unit." He paused and waited for the officers to give him their attention. They stopped bantering Malik and stared up at him. "Officer Lee, Officer Robinson, Officer Bond, and Walker, and last but not least, Malik will get the last laugh on you all because he, with the others, has been promoted to detective and will be working undercover in narcotics."

Malik's drooped body came to full attention. He stared at the Sergeant as if in disbelief. Surely it was a joke and any minute

Washburn would admit as much. He could feel all eyes in the room on him. He never made a request for undercover work and knew the other officers were probably wondering how he, of all people, could work undercover. He was too soft for that kind of high-level intrigue and danger. Malik waited for Washburn to bust out laughing, but he didn't.

Instead, he said, "Congratulations, gentlemen, the lieutenant from CI will be contacting you as to when they want you to report for your new assignment. Again, congratulations and be safe out there today. Roll call is over."

Malik sat dumbfounded. He tried to ignore the taunts from the older officers who filed by him on their way out.

"You ain't got no business in the detective unit," the first officer who commented on his not getting promoted earlier said. "You're still learning patrol."

"You rookie," another officer taunted. "Good luck, but I doubt you'll last a day in undercover."

"Yeah, he'll be so nervous that he'll give himself away," a third man added.

"Now you'll get a chance to throw some real bad guys under the jail where they belong," still another officer said and then laughed. The men giving him a hard time patted each other on the back as they left the room.

Malik sat there as the afternoon shift of police officers left the room, leaving him alone to think further about what had just happened to him. Undercover work meant busting drug dealers, something he didn't mind doing. After all, they were a real menace to the Black community with no conscience and no concern for the damage they were doing to his people. But he preferred to be at the other end of the process, which is saving the youth from becoming drug dealers and especially drug users.

Malik knew he would be good at mentoring young brothers who had no role models in their lives and often no hope for the future according to how they viewed life. Why hadn't they given him an assignment for which he was best suited and where he could help prevent crime instead of fighting crime? Because he loved police work, he would accept this assignment, but would still look for the day when he could serve his community in a more positive role. In the meantime, he would go undercover and fight the bad guys just like in the movies.

Malik slowly pulled himself out of the chair and strolled out of the roll call room. He picked up his pace as he headed down the long corridor toward the cafeteria. Before leaving for the day's assignment he always bought an Evian water. His thoughts were still on what had just happened when Lieutenant Wendell Hampton, head of the Criminal Investigation Unit approached him.

"Welcome aboard," Hampton said as he slapped Malik on the back. "We're glad to have you join us in C.I. I've heard good things about you."

What good things could he have possibly heard about me? Malik wondered. He hadn't done any more than any other beat officer. It was probably just part of the con game. Make him feel good and say things that would force him to perform at a higher standard. By telling him that good things were being said about him would force Malik to live up to the hype.

"Thanks, Lieutenant," Malik replied. "Glad to be aboard."

"I'm taking you off patrol immediately," Hampton said. "How about you take the next two weeks off. Just relax and get ready for the change, you know, like grow your hair out, change up your appearance, and start to look a little gruffy." Hampton placed his hand on Malik's shoulder. "You'll get a five-hundred-dollar clothing allowance. You're going to be back in the middle of the hood on the other side of the law so buy clothes that fit the environment." Hampton tapped Malik on the shoulder and then moved back a few steps. Go on and take off. When we see you back here be ready for another couple week's training and then your first assignment. How does that sound to you?"

"Sounds just great," Malik answered with little enthusiasm.

"Good, son. I'll let your Sergeant know you're being transferred immediately and won't be working your shift today. Stop by tomorrow and see Sergeant Hall so you can get your undercover vehicle." Hampton finished, turned, and called out to Sergeant Washburn. "Hold up, Sarge, I need to talk to you. We're pulling Malik off his beat today. He's now officially transferred to CI."

Malik watched as Hampton caught up with Sergeant Washburn and the two men disappeared around the corner. Hampton's words to Washburn reverberated over and over again with Malik. He really had been transferred to undercover, but he didn't quite understand why. What was it in his behavior or his performance for the past three years that convinced these men that he would serve the department better putting criminals in jail? And many of these criminals would be just like many of his friends he grew up in Cleveland. Many of these young men that he would send to long prison terms had never gotten a decent break in life and turned to a life of crime as their only option. What they really needed was a mentor to help them understand who they were and their worth as young men. But instead, they would get a long prison sentence and the system wouldn't have to worry about them at all. That's not what he wanted to do, but at this point, Malik had no choice. How long he could do this kind of dirty work he just didn't know.

The next morning Malik pulled into a parking space at the police warehouse right at eight o'clock. As he got out of his car, he watched the large metal door swing open. He spotted Sergeant Hall, chief of the warehouse, on the other side.

"Congratulations, I hear you made detective." Hall greeted Malik.

"Sure did," Malik replied. He walked into the large warehouse and shook the Sergeant's hand.

"Man, you going to be working undercover in narcotics," Sergeant Hall continued. He patted Malik on the back and walked toward the area where the undercover vehicles were stored. "You go for the exciting and dangerous kind of action, don't you?"

If only he knew, Malik thought. "It beats writing traffic tickets on little old ladies, who most of the time shouldn't be driving anyway." Malik stared at the twenty various models of cars parked in three rows. He felt like a kid in the candy store. He could pick any one of the twenty. What a decision.

He spotted a black Nissan Maxima with twenty-inch chrome rims and blacked out tinted windows.

"Can I have this one?"

"I don't see why not. We can do up the paperwork real quick and get it assigned to you."

"Yeah, Sarge this is the one I want."

"Well, let's get it done."

The two men walked back to Sergeant Hall's office. He grabbed some papers off the shelf behind his desk, sat down at his desk, and started filling them out. Malik sat across from him with a sense of anxiety. This was really happening and for the first time, he felt a tinge of excitement. This was not what he wanted to do, but since he had to do it, why not find some enjoyment in it?

Sergeant Hall slid the papers across the desk and handed Malik a pen. "Sign where I put the checkmarks," he said.

Malik took the pen and signed his name in four different boxes and slid the paperwork back across the desk.

"Okay you're all set," Sergeant Hall said as he took his pen back from Malik, separated the papers, folded one set, and handed them to Malik. "If the vehicle gets burnt, bring it back to the warehouse and we'll trade it out for another model." He stood up. "If the vehicle doesn't get burnt, you can still change it out in three months. You know, nothing like a little variety, free of charge."

The two men walked over to the car and Hall handed Malik the keys. "Good luck and be safe out there."

"Thanks, Sarge." Malik opened the door and climbed in the driver's seat. He smiled as he ran his hand over the smooth tan leather upholstery. The car was loaded with a Bose sound system and upgraded woofers, and a television in the headrest and dash. Malik started out of the garage and headed to the mall. He had one more chore and that was to buy some new clothes to match his new position. With the five hundred the department gave him, he was about to make that transition.

The department gave Malik two weeks of uncharged leave in order to allow him to grow a beard, let his hair grow long, and allow for mental preparation. During the two weeks, he spent a lot of time meditating on this life-changing experience he was about to undergo. He also spent time with his girlfriend, Jonetta. She was adamantly opposed to the change and had no problem expressing her dissatisfaction. One night over dinner their relationship almost came to a breaking point.

"This isn't fair," she scowled while sipping on a Margarita. "I guess I'll just have to accept the fact that your job is more important to you than our future."

"Don't say that, because it just isn't true." Malik reached across the table and tried to take her hand.

She jerked her hand away and slid it under the table. "You didn't think enough about me to discuss making this change. You just did it."

"It's not what I wanted, Jonetta. You know that."

"But it's what you accepted."

"I didn't have a choice. You turn down a promotion and it'll be a long time before you get another offer."

"I don't want you working for the stupid police anyway. All you going to be doing is sending our Black kids to jail. Doesn't that bother you at all?"

Malik reared way back in his chair. Maybe his decision to accept this job didn't make any sense because he did agree with Jonetta. Their love of kids and their shared concern for young Blacks were what attracted them to each other. He knew she never would have agreed to a relationship with a policeman if he hadn't convinced her that he viewed the job as a way to help save boys who were victims of the pathological environment they lived in. She had believed him when he told her that as soon as he was eligible for a transfer to community service work, he would do it. And now he had to convince her that was still his intentions when his actions pointed in the opposite direction. He didn't want to lose Jonetta and in fact, he planned to marry her once he achieved the financial stability so that she wouldn't have to work if she didn't want to.

"Are you listening to me or am I just talking to myself?" Jonetta's harsh words ended Malik's musing.

"Yes, sweetheart, I hear you," he said. "But wouldn't you agree that some of our boys need to be locked up?" He scooted in closer. "Don't get me wrong. I know our boys get a bum rap in life, but we can't let the ones who blame everything on the system or the white man and use that as an excuse to rob, steal, and sometimes kill other kids spoil it for the rest. It's important that we save the potentially good ones, but there is also a bunch beyond saving. As long as I have to do this kind of work, those will be the ones I'll go after."

He noticed his explanation seemed to relax Jonetta.

"Just as long as you don't forget that," she said in a much softer tone.

Malik got up and walked around the table, leaned down, and kissed Jonetta on the forehead.

"I won't," he said. "I promise you that I won't." He walked back to his chair and sat down. "Let's order."

****

A surge of excitement shot through Malik's emotionally charged body as he pulled the Maxima into one of the many parking spaces reserved for 'Detectives Only." It made him feel special. He was now a part of a select cadre of law enforcement officers. Reserved parking was one of the privileges that went along with that selective category. Malik had to check himself or he could really begin to enjoy the special attention that he was about to get.

He entered the headquarters building at 8:00, but was stopped before he got through the door by a security guard.

"Hey, you, this is for police officers only," the guard said gruffly. "What do you want?"

Malik smiled and flashed his badge at the guard.

"Malik, is that you?" the guard asked.

"Yeah, it's me, Smitty."

"Man, you sure look different. What happened?"

"Special assignment. I've been moved to undercover so I had to alter my appearance and no more uniforms."

"You did one heck of a job," the guard said with a broad smile. "You sure fooled me."

"Isn't that the nature of what I'm going to be doing?" Malik asked rhetorically. "Fooling people?"

"You know you right." The guard raised his hand and Malik slapped it and then went inside.

As he strolled down the long corridor, other officers stared at him. Evidently, they also didn't recognize him. The more it seemed that he could fool people who actually knew him with his altered appearance, the more secure he felt about going out into the community. If he could get over this easily on trained policemen, he sure would be able to do the same out in the world.

Malik made it to his new home, the Criminal Investigation Unit of Detectives. When he entered the office, his new sergeant seemed to be waiting for him.

"Good morning detective," Sergeant greeted him. "It's amazing what two weeks can do. You sure don't look like Patrolman Williams anymore." The Sergeant got up, reached across the desk, and shook Malik's hand.

"You think I'll fit in okay out there with the criminal element?" he asked.

"You'll do just fine. Just remember though, you're one of the good guys."

"No problem," Malik said in a terse tone. He kind of resented the implication. He watched as the Sergeant reached in his desk and pulled out a detective's gold badge.

"Let me have that patrolman's badge," he said.

Malik handed him the patrolman's badge and took his new one.

"That should make you feel real special," the Sergeant said.

"It does."

"Are you ready?"

"As I'll ever be."

The sergeant placed his arm around Malik's shoulder and they both headed out of the room.

"Good 'cause the next two weeks I'm going to train you to be the best undercover detective in this unit."

Sergeant wasn't kidding about the training. It was two weeks of the most intense work Malik had ever encountered. But when he finished and finally reported to work that evening for the real thing, he was ready. Working in community service was now behind him. He was anxious to get out in the field and test his newly acquired skills. The Friday of his last day of training, he was told exactly what he'd be doing. When he arrived at headquarters, he met up with Detective Wendell Booker, the man he was replacing.

"I hear you came through the training with flying colors," Booker greeted him.

"I guess I did all right," Malik replied.

"Let's get going into the real world," Booker said as the two men headed toward the Maxima. "Fun and games are now over. You're getting ready to play in the big leagues and face some real major league criminals. And remember no errors." Booker paused for a moment as he climbed into the passenger seat and fastened his seat belt. "In this game, errors will get you killed."

Malik climbed behind the wheel and they started off into a place where there was a possibility there would be no return. They drove the five blocks south out of the downtown area and turned left onto Martin Luther King Boulevard. What a contrast just a few blocks could make. They'd left the busy downtown area with its tall buildings, people dressed in business suits hurrying into their offices, with brand new cars filling the streets and entered an area with rundown boarded-up storefronts. Trash was strewn across the streets, and there was dirt where there should have been grass. Within a three-block area, they passed three pawn shops, two liquor stores, and two older storefront buildings. One of the buildings had a worn-out marquee with the words, JERUSALEM BAPTIST CHURCH: COME HERE AND FIND JESUS, REVEREND WILLIE JACKSON, PASTOR. A couple blocks further down Martin Luther King Boulevard, Malik saw another run-down building serving as a church. The glass in the marquee was broken. It also had a message to the passersby: "COME FIND JESUS. HE IS YOUR HOPE AND SALVATION, BETHEL BAPTIST CHURCH, DR. PASTOR ROSCOE ANDERSON, MINISTER."

Malik looked back at the road just in time to slam on his brakes, stopping in front of a disheveled man who had staggered out into the street. He glared over at Booker, and they both shook their heads.

"It never ends," Booker said.

"And I wonder will it ever?" Malik asked.

"I don't know," Booker said and then jerked his head to the right. "Hey, there's our man standing over there in that Church's Fried Chicken parking lot. Pull in over there."

"You sure this guy is all right?" Malik asked as he stared at a dark-skinned man who looked to be six feet tall, very thin, and about thirty years old. He had a clean-shaven head, imitation diamond earrings in each ear. He wore black slacks and a shirt with rundown black shoes.

"Been a snitch for me for over three years. He knows his way around. Claims he's not hustling anymore. But I believe he's turned informant as a way to get rid of his competition."

"Real nice guy, huh?"

"He's not trying to be nice. Just trying to hustle," Booker said. "Pull over there to that parking space." He pointed to an empty space facing the boulevard inside the church's parking lot.

Malik followed Booker's instructions and pulled the Maxima into an open space.

"I'm going to turn him over to you. I got no need for him since I'm finished with undercover. His name is Mello and he's going to test you." Booker hit the button and the window rolled down. "So, put him in his place right off and it's okay to joke a little with these guys, but never, not ever trust them, and always let them know who is in charge." He finished and called out. "Mello, over here."

Mello stared over at Booker and then Malik. His brows furrowed as he hesitated before making a move.

"He's trying to figure out what's going on," Booker said. "He's really checking you out. Wouldn't you hate to live this life? Never knowing who to trust and always suspicious. Sometimes you wonder how these guys ever sleep."

"Maybe they don't," Malik said as he stared at Mello. There was nothing really different about him. He looked like any other Black man hanging out in a fast-food parking lot with no job and nothing to do all day but find ways to hustle. For Black men like him, hustling was a full-time job. Malik knew this same scene was playing out all over this country in every inner city. Given a different set of circumstances and a different break in life, Mello might have been a banker or president of some large corporation. Instead, he was a hustler.

"Get over here," Booker shouted. "I ain't got all day to deal with you. It's all good."

Mello sauntered over to the driver's side and glared inside.

"Get in the back," Booker instructed him.

"Who is this guy?" Mello asked as he looked at Malik.

"Your new contact. Now get in."

Mello hesitated for another minute and then got in the backseat right behind Booker.

"Let's get out of here," Booker said.

"Where to?" Malik asked.

"Don't matter, just drive anywhere." Booker turned back toward Mello, handed him a package, and continued. "This is your new inside contact. His name is Malik."

Momentarily, Malik took his eyes off the road and extended his hand back to Mello.

"How you be?" he asked.

Mello slapped his hand. "I'm here," he said, then snatched his arm back and turned directly to Booker. "So, we got a new green hornet? I don't know if I can work with no young buck."

"What's up with this fool?" Malik blurted out. "What makes this loser think I want to work him?" He abruptly pulled over to the curb, slammed on the brakes. "In fact, get this fool out my car."

Just as abruptly as he stopped, he hit the gas, and the car jerked at high speed back onto the street. "No, as a matter of fact, let's drop this fool off right in the middle of the hood, so when we put him out everybody going to know he's a snitch."

Booker broke out in a hearty laugh. "That'll work for me." He turned and looked back at his snitch. "I'm finished with him, so it's up to you, partner. If you don't think you can work with him, we might as well give him back to the dealers he's been snitching on."

"Y'all stop foolin' around," Mello scowled. "That ain't one bit funny."

Malik now had Mello's attention. He pulled over to the curb, turned, and looked back at the snitch.

"Now you ready to put the work in?" he asked.

"Yeah, man, let's do it."

"Tell me what you got?" Booker asked.

"Five young boys, bout nineteen or twenty sellin' out of three houses, side by side." Mello leaned forward in the backseat.

The snitch definitely was ready to put work in, Malik thought.

"I can buy directly from the stash house where they're holding most of the drugs instead of from the runners," Mello continued.

"How you figure that?" Malik asked. He was really feeling it now.

"'Cause I go by there and know the head man."

"How tough a bust will it be?" Booker now asked.

"They got the usual security. Plenty of young boys with walkie-talkies all up and down the street and hiding in the bushes. Or they just might be sittin' on the porches of other houses all along the block." Mello relaxed back in the seat. "When you do the raid you goin' have to hit 'em quick."

"Okay, let's check them out," Booker said. "Drive back behind that alley." He pointed to an alley near the spot where they were parked.

Malik pulled out, drove over to the alley, and parked.

"You know the exercise," Booker said to Mello. "Out of the car."

All three men got out of the car, and Malik patted Mello down for drugs.

"He's clean," he said.

"Good," Booker said. "Now give us everything in your pockets. You go in there clean."

Mello emptied his pockets and gave all the contents to Malik, who then pulled out a twenty-dollar bill and gave it to the snitch.

"Let's go," Booker said.

They got back in the car and Malik drove back to within a couple of blocks of the drug houses. Mello jumped out the back seat and hustled down the street to the drug house.

Malik and Booker watched Mello disappear around the corner heading toward the drug house. They waited for fifteen minutes.

"Head over to Third Street. We'll pick him up over there," Booker said. "Don't drive past the stash house. Go up a couple of blocks and then come back around."

"You got it," Malik followed instructions. He finally made it to Third Street, where Mello waited on the corner. He jumped in the backseat and Malik drove back to the alley and parked.

"What you got?" Booker asked while thrusting his open hand back toward Mello.

He put a small bag with a white rock-like substance in Booker's hand.

"What's it like in there?" Booker asked as he put the bag in his jacket pocket.

"There are four young boys inside. The main one is a young brother they call Tech. His real name is Eric Johnson and he's about eighteen. It's his mamma's house, but she wasn't nowhere around. She works at night as a nurse's aide and she actually has a daycare there during the day." Mello reared back and relaxed. "All them kids up in there during the day and their mammas don't know right in that same house they running drugs at night.' He laughed as though it was funny and then continued. "When I went in Tech was sitting there cutting up a half key.

"Wait a minute," Malik interrupted. "You say it's his mamma's house and they run a daycare out of there during the day?"

"Yeah, that's right," Mello answered.

"You mean this fool is stashing and selling drugs right out of his mother's house with all those kids there during the day?"

"That's right," Mello said. "They all do it when they're that young and in the game. That's where they get started. Right under their mamma's eyes."

"You sure she wasn't in there?" Malik continued.

"No way. They do it during the hours their mamas are at work. When she gets home, they just close down the operation."

"You're telling me their mothers know nothing about what's going on?"

"They don't know until it's too late."

"There are no fathers?"

Mello broke out laughing. "Be serious. You all done already locked up the daddies. Then you do the sons. These boys think their daddies are heroes. You know like real men who took on the system."

"And lost."

"These boys don't see it that way. Prison is a rite of passage for them. Shows you're not afraid of the man's system and you'll take it on at all cost."

Malik now turned and looked at Booker.

"What'll happen to the mother after the bust?" he asked.

"Depends," Booker replied. "If she didn't know what was going on, nothing, but if we find out she was a part of it or even getting money from the sales, she could go down just like the rest of them." Booker paused for a moment, then turned his attention back to Mello. "Okay, let's wrap this up." He pulled out a fifty-dollar bill and handed it to Booker. "This is for your work."

"When you going to take them down?" Mello asked as he took the money and stuffed it in his pocket.

"Next two or three days, or when we know they just re-upped," Booker said. "I'll contact you. I want you to go down with the bust."

Malik stared over at Booker. "You want him to get busted, too?"

"Yeah," Booker answered. "We want him in the wagon so he can tell us what they talk about. That's the best time to catch them telling on each other and naming bigger fish to fry while they're scared about what's going to happen to them."

"I'll be ready," Mello said, opened the door and exited the car.

"What a piece of junk," Malik mumbled as he pulled back out into traffic.

"Don't be so hard on the brother," Booker said. "He's critical to our operation. Without him, it'd be much harder to bust this riff-raff. Let's get back to the station, test this rock, and get our warrants ready for signature."

Malik and Booker rode in silence. As he followed the flow of traffic down Martin Luther King Boulevard, Malik's thoughts focused on the nature of the work he'd gotten himself into and the kind of people he'd be dealing with on a regular basis. Mello was a low-life, dirtbag with no value system and no morals at all. There were so many out there just like him that it disgusted Malik. There are two different worlds operating within the context of one America. There is that world operating above the surface of law and order. There are millions of Americans who live what is considered a normal life. Then there is that world existing below the surface of legality, where nothing is considered normal except for those who live in it. Cheating, lying, stealing, and even murder is normal behavior to that America. Instead of going to college, they go to jail and instead of going to work, they go to court. Their boss is a judge who has total control over their lives. What frightened Malik is the fact that the world seemed to be winning the battle for the hearts and minds of young Blacks who admire drug dealers, because, according to their thinking, the dealer is getting over on the system. He is beating the man.

Malik shook his head as he pulled into the station's parking lot. He and Booker went straight to the evidence lab and had the rock tested. The results came back positive for crack cocaine.

"It's the real thing," Booker said. "Now all we have to do is execute the warrant and we'll put another group of these little punks away for a very long time."

"Yeah," Malik replied. "I'll catch up with you later," he said to Booker and headed to the restroom. He needed to clean up and get the filth off him. He needed to wash away the ugliness of what probably could never be washed clean.

A nervous Malik paced back and forth in the assembly area of headquarters. It had been a long day and now would be a very long night as all the SWAT teams assembled for the bust scheduled to go down at ten o'clock that night. Earlier in the day Mello called and told him that Tech received a big shipment of drugs that morning. He happened to be there when it arrived. Mello had really won the confidence of Tech to the point that he transacted his business right in front of him.

Once Malik received that tip, he notified Lieutenant Bronson, who in turn, organized the SWAT teams. He watched the men come into the room wearing all black army pants, black desert boots, black drug unit jackets with the words SWAT TEAM in bright orange on the back, and black Ninja masks. They carried nine-millimeter Smith and Wesson semi-automatic pistols with two members armed with shotguns. He was awestruck at the overwhelming display of power. He felt ambivalent about what was about to happen. Young brothers who dabbled in the illicit drug business had to be brought down. At the least they were a menace to the community where they conducted their sick kind of business, and at most, they killed people, either through the drugs or directly if they happened to get in their way. The other side of him harbored a deep-seated concern for the chaos and pain it caused the community in general and specifically the families of the boys who, once busted, would be forced to confront the prospect of a long time behind bars.

"Listen up," Bronson called out. "We got three houses to hit. Team one, you got twelve men and you'll be taking down the stash house, which is the place where they keep all the money and distribute the drugs. The main man will be in there. There'll probably be four other young men inside with him. Be careful and don't take any chances because they'll be armed with automatic weapons. Search and secure the premises." Bronson handed Malik a diagram of the house. He'd gotten the diagram to the insides of all three houses from a computer search. "This is a two-story house so make sure you search both floors thoroughly." Bronson paused for a second and smiled. "Do one of our patented re-decorating jobs on the interior."

Malik took the diagram and the other members of his team gathered around him to study it.

"Team two, you got twelve men and you'll take down the house to the left of the stash house. Team three you'll secure the house to the right. These are both distribution houses, and there'll be anywhere from four to six runners in there. Might be some crack heads inside buying drugs. Take everybody down.

Afterward, we'll sort out who is who. That's not really our job. Let the District Attorney deal with that." He handed two more diagrams to the men in charge of the two teams. "Those are both one-story houses, but pretty much empty since they both are abandoned. Still search them thoroughly."

Finally, Bronson turned to team four. "You know your job. Takedown and detain anyone out and about on the street. Hold them down until the area is secure and it can be determined they had no involvement with the drug activity from the targeted locations."

Bronson stopped for a couple of minutes and allowed the teams to review the diagrams and talk.

"According to Malik's snitch, they have lookouts up and down the street with walkie-talkies warning our targeted locations of any suspicious activity outside. To counter them we have to hit quick and fast. We'll jam the frequency they are believed to be using. To throw them off, we'll roll up on them in a U-Haul truck." Again, Bronson paused and smiled. "We plan to haul something, but it ain't furniture. You'll deploy from the rear of the truck on signal from Sergeant Dowe who'll be your driver. Since we know they have weapons, we got a no-knock nighttime search warrant. When you get to the targets, take the doors off the hinges with a ram and swarm in like a pool of flesh-eating fish. Make them sorry they ever dealt a drug or got up that morning. Put the fear of our awesome power in them. Let them know this is our world and this is a losing game. Any questions?"

Fifty men held their weapons high in the air and in unison shouted, "Yeah!"

An hour and a half after the SWAT teams left the station they pulled back in with their prisoners, including Mello who was busted right outside the stash house. Malik was impressed with how smoothly the bust went, with no glitches. Each team followed the game plan and those boys didn't know what hit them. They arrested Tech and four Black teenagers, along with $20,000, five handguns, and two kilos of cocaine in the stash house. From the second and third houses, they secured six young men, all Black between the ages of fourteen and eighteen, five handguns, and one ounce of cocaine. Ten Black men standing outside or around the houses were taken in for having crack cocaine in their possession and a couple had weapons. By any measurement criteria, Malik's first bust had been a success.

Along with four other men, Malik packaged and logged all the drugs and the money into evidence. For that moment, he was the hero, receiving accolades from every officer in the building.

"Malik, great job," one officer said and patted him on the back.

"Man, you sure learned the game fast," another said.

"Hey Malik, thanks for busting that bunch of trash. Too bad you didn't get a chance to take a few of them out," was the response from another man.

His words caused Malik to cringe. He actually wanted them to kill some of these young men. The thought sickened him. He had made a difference, but was it something to be proud of, he just didn't know. The images of those boys' heads bent and in cuffs stayed with him. He had busted kids between the ages of fourteen and eighteen and now their lives were all but ruined. And as quickly as he took that bunch off the street, there would be another bunch to replace them. He finished logging the evidence in and had one more job to do before he could call it a night.

Mello had been removed and placed in a holding cell away from the others. Malik made it down to his cell, unlocked it, and waved him out.

"Good bust," is all he could think to say to this man who he disliked.

"Yeah, and there'll be a lot more in the future," Mello said as he walked out of the cell.

Malik slammed it shut and the two of them walked back into the main area of the police headquarters. They headed outside and Malik handed Mello a package with $2,000 inside.

"For your efforts," Malik said.

"I appreciate your generosity," Mello replied and tucked the money in his pocket. "But let me get out of here. I don't want to push my luck 'cause ain't no tellin' who might be driving by here to see what they can find out. Every dealer out there knows what went down by now and they'll be checking to see if they can put it all together. And I sure don't want them to find out I was the one."

"Makes sense," Malik said tersely. He really didn't like talking to this lowlife, but knew he had no choice. That was the nature of the business. "I'll be in touch."

"You do that." Mello put his hands in his pockets and strolled away.

Malik watched Mello as he disappeared around the corner. Instead of going back inside the building to get to the rear parking lot, he decided to walk outside. He wasn't in the mood for any more accolades or "that-a-boys" and high fives. The energy rush he experienced during the preparation and the actual bust right up to watching Mello put his hands in his pocket and turn the corner had dissipated and now Malik felt a bit depressed.

He made it to the back of the building and practically ran to his car. He didn't want to see any more policemen, he didn't want to see any more young Black kids cuffed and heads bowed, a symbol of their demise, and he sure didn't want to see anyone like Mello at that time. Malik needed no reminders of the kind of people he was dealing with on a daily basis.

He looked at his watch. It read one o'clock and there were very few cars on the street. But there was one particular car that stayed a little distance behind him and it made him nervous. As he neared his home, he decided not to pull in the driveway, but instead kept going to the corner, made a right turn, and went back on the expressway. He wanted to make sure the car wasn't following him. The driver did not turn; the car kept going straight. Malik smiled at the irony of it all. He was behaving in much the same manner as the drug dealers. Paranoia was settling in as he imagined every car behind him full of young thugs just waiting for the opportunity to put a bullet in his head. He needed to chill out. He grabbed his cell phone and dialed a number in Cleveland.

"Hey, Dad."

"That you, Malik?"

"Yeah."

"How's it going, Son? Everything all right? Something gone wrong on the new assignment?"

"It's going. How are you and Mom?"

"We're fine, but you didn't call this time of night just to find out how we're doing. What's going on?"

"I'm not sure I like what I'm doing," Malik lowered his voice as if someone might be listening. His paranoia was kicking in again.

"You don't like doing that undercover stuff?"

"I have to admit I got mixed feelings about it and what some of those feelings are I don't like."

"What is it? Can you pinpoint it?" His dad's voice rose a bit.

"I like the power and prestige and I don't know if that is a good thing. I felt a surge of incredible power this evening when I participated in my first bust. But then when I saw the end result, which was about twenty young Black kids between the ages of fourteen and eighteen with their lives wrecked, I felt guilty." He paused but his dad said nothing. "Don't get me wrong, what these boys are doing is dead wrong and it has to be stopped. But they aren't anything but pawns for a much larger game organized at a level we'll probably never touch. I don't know if what I'm doing will really make a difference."

"It affected you that badly?"

"I think it's changing me. And I don't think the end justifies the means. A police raid is brutal, not only on the criminals, but the entire neighborhood."

"Son, don't lose your identity of who you are. Let the job become you, not you becoming the job. If you ever want a good laugh, Son, ask someone when you meet them who they are and the first thing they tell you is the title of their job." Now it was his father's turn to pause. Malik knew why. He was letting his advice sink in, something he'd done with Malik all his life. "You are someone who loves to help people—especially kids, you love family, and you're a humanitarian. You are someone who wants to make a difference. As long as you can remember that and never let them change you, then you'll survive this. You'll have to take tough but firm stands when confronted, but just remember it takes more courage for a man to be true to himself than for a soldier to fight on the battlefield."

"You're right, Dad."

"Just stay true to yourself, Son."

"I'll talk to you later, and I love you."

"Love you, too, Son."

Over the next two weeks, Malik was on a roll. Mello introduced him to five new players in the game and he was buying directly from them. Malik also had five new informants on the payroll and the number kept growing. The very ones that didn't seem like good prospects to snitch turned out to be the main ones. They were ready to set up friends and even family members in order to stay out of jail. His success had swollen his ego to the point that it had all but silenced his heart. He was on a high, unlike any drug. And he was also developing the "us" against "them" mentality of the other members of the team, the one trait he'd disliked about the others.

Malik had been so good in such a short period of time that Lieutenant Bronson decided to send him into the most infected drug area of the city, Dupont Housing Project. It happened to be the area where he had originally been assigned when on police duty and where he wanted to do community service. Since he'd spent so much time in there before, he had to alter his looks even more than in the past. His beard grew thicker and longer, and he had dreadlocks. He wore a red, black, and green cap covering the back part of his head and the dreadlocks flowed out from under it. Knowing the area quite well, he knew his first task would be to establish a contact with someone so that he wouldn't appear suspicious. That neighborhood did not like outsiders just hanging around.

He pulled into the complex in his Maxima with the music blaring a Tupac rap song. About a half dozen young brothers standing on the corner eyeballed him and he knew what they were thinking. He needed to make contact with someone real quick. He spotted a young, slim lady, about five-feet-two and quite pretty. He rolled down the window and called out.

"Whuz up, baby girl?"

"What's up with you?" she replied. "Who you out here to see?"

"You, now." Malik smiled.

"Whatever, boy."

"For real, but you look like one of those heart breakers, so I don't think I should step to you."

"That's you, playa."

Malik knew he was making good progress. "Come sit with ya boy and talk unless you got a man out here." He gestured for her to come around to the passenger side of the car.

She smiled and strolled around to the passenger side of the car, leaned down, and placed her arms on the car. "Myself, I'm living the single life."

"Well get in and let's see if I can win your heart."

She opened the door and slid into the passenger's seat.

Malik could now relax as the young men who had been watching his every action turned their attention away from him. They assumed that he was there to see the girl. He turned his attention back to her.

"What's your name, Shorty?"

"My friends call me Mae," she said with one of the prettiest smiles Malik had ever seen. This was one beautiful person.

"My name is Malik and I sure am glad I just happened to be driving down this street and saw you walking your fine self down it."

"Are you a playa or what?"

"Nah, baby girl. I'm just a hustler trying to make that money. You got a problem with that?"

"That's cool, whatever you got to do to make that money."

"I'm just trying to come up. You ain't in the game are you, baby girl?"

"Nah, but I know a lot brothas out here that are. But they cool. I grew up with most of them."

"For real, 'cause I just got out here a few months ago and I need to make some contacts. But they have to be moving some weight, you know, no nickel and dime stuff."

"Ones I know are heavy hitters."

"Cool, that's what I'm talking about, a ride-and-die chick."

"Nah, I don't usually get down like that. But I think you're kind of cute, so I'll hook you up with them.

"At least I know these brothas ain't going to try to rob me if they cool with you." Malik reached over and ran his hand along the contours of Mae's face. She didn't resist. "You eat yet?"

"Nah, you gonna treat me to something?"

"For sure. How about some Red Lobster?"

"That'll work for me. Let's go."

Malik pulled away from the curb and headed out of the projects. He pulled out his cell phone and called his surveillance team and pretended to be talking to his cousin.

"Yo, what up, cuz? Hey I met this shorty out at the Dupont and we about to go get some Red Lobster. After we eat and I drop her back off, I'll get up with you then. I'll holla at you later." He closed the phone, stuck it in his pocket, and turned his attention back to Mae. "You sure one fine sistah. How someone fine as you walking around without a man?"

"'Cause these brothas, they be trippin'. You know, tryin' too much to be possessive."

"Yeah, ain't nothin' worse than an insecure brotha. It's cool; ain't no pressure here. It's whatever day-by-day. I don't like all that drama myself. Life's too short for all that."

"Ain't it, though?"

Malik laughed. "I see we going to get along real good." Malik pulled into the Red Lobster parking lot, they got out and strolled into the restaurant.

They found a table near the window so they could look out at the trees that lined the side of the building. The waitress approached them and put two menus on the table.

"How y'all doing this evening?" she asked as she pulled out her order pad and pencil. "You ready to order or do you need a little time?"

"I don't know about you, but I'm starving," Malik said as he picked up the menu and opened it.

"I know what I want," Mae said.

"And what is that?" Malik asked.

Mae looked up at the waitress. "I'll have the wood–grilled sirloin surf and turf with ice tea."

"Good choice," Malik said. "The lady has good taste." He looked up at the waitress. "The lobster lover's dream for me."

"What to drink?" the waitress asked.

"Raspberry lemonade," Malik answered.

"I'll bring your drinks right away and get your orders in also." The waitress turned and walked away.

They spent the next two hours talking and enjoying their meal. Malik constantly reminded Mae that he needed those introductions as soon as possible. She assured him it would happen and when they finished, he signaled the waitress over to his table. Malik pulled a large wad of money out, peeled off a hundred-dollar bill to cover the meal and another hundred dollars for the waitress.

"You ready to make a move, baby girl?"

"Yeah, but aren't you going to wait for your change?"

"What change?"

"Yo, you got it like that?" Mae said and smiled.

As they strolled out of the restaurant, Malik knew he'd made the kind of impression on Mae that would assure him of meeting those contacts.

Malik parked in front of Mae's apartment unit. No doubt she was attracted to him and this could go further. But at all cost, he had to avoid any kind of intimacy with her. He got out and walked her up to her apartment.

"Can I get that number?" he asked as she reached for her key.

"849-2016," she reeled it off quickly.

He knew Mae was waiting for him to ask to come in. She cracked the door open. He had to think fast. He grabbed his cell phone and faked dialing a number.

"Dre, what's up? I'm about to spend some time with a beautiful young lady. Anything I need to know?" He frowned, moved the phone from his ear acting like he just heard some terrible news. "What?" he shouted.

Just as Mae opened the door, he said. "Mae, I got to go. Something's happened to my cuz and I've got to get over there." He gave Mae a hug. "I'll call you later." He then ran to his car, swung the door open and jumped inside.

As he pulled out onto the street, he smiled. He was getting pretty good at this and it gave him quite a rush.

The next day Malik drove into the Dupont Projects and parked in front of Mae's apartment complex. Six young men stood around the outside of the apartments drinking and smoking.

"Whuz up, playas?" he shouted

"That's you, dawg. I can't call it," one of the men answered.

Malik laughed as he walked up to Mae's door and knocked.

"Who is it?"

"Malik, open the door."

The door swung open and Mae looked just as stunning as she had the day before.

"Come on in," she said softly. "I've been trying to study for my upcoming exams." She walked back over to a small dining room table covered with papers and books and sat down. He followed her over and sat across from her.

Seeing all those books stunned him. "Studying?" he asked. "Studying for what?"

"For my upcoming exams, silly."

"You go to school?"

"No, I go to college. I'm getting my degree in Business Management with a concentration in Information Management."

Malik was speechless. "How much time do you have before you get your degree?" he finally asked.

"One more year and I'll be graduating.'

"So, you're trying to do something, huh?"

"Yeah, I'm definitely trying to get it together. I want to get up out of here," she said as she began to arrange the books and papers in front of her. "Malik, I'm from a family that's three generations in these projects. My mother lives in the building next door and my grandparents live two buildings down. Not to mention I've lost three cousins and two uncles to these projects. I just want a better life for me and my daughter."

"You got a daughter? How old is she?"

"She's going on three," Mae stopped moving papers and looked across at Malik. "She's at my mom's since I've been studying for my finals." She sat straight up in her chair and all her attention was on Malik. "I'm going to let you know that I'm going to introduce you to these dealers out there that I grew up with. But don't you ever bring that junk in my house or around me. It's just something about you I don't know what it is, but your eyes tell me you're really a good person. It's like you're out here hustlin' but it's not really you. I guess that's what I really like about you. Your eyes don't lie about who you are. They reveal your soul." She stopped and smiled.

The more she talked, the more Malik realized that he was getting in deeper than what was safe. He had to change the subject. One of the cardinal rules of his work was no personal attachment with the enemy and she, at that point, was the enemy.

"So, what are my eyes saying now?" he asked as he looked up and down her.

She laughed. "Boy, you so silly. Can't you ever be serious?"

He was acting rather silly, but his mind was on a serious problem. Once Mae introduced him to her friends to buy drugs, she would become a conspirator and be locked up for conspiracy. It would be his fault. He would have used her and taken advantage of her need to find someone she could believe in and care for. It was so much easier to consider using Mae to infiltrate when he knew nothing about her. However, now it was too late to back off.

"Come on, let's walk across the way so I can introduce you to Kenny," Mae said interrupting his musing.

Yes, it was too late, he thought, as he followed her out of the apartment.

They walked across the yard into another apartment and started up the stairs to the second floor. As they started down the hall three young brothers came out of one of the apartments and walked toward them. The brother in the middle a very thin, tall brother seemed to be the leader.

"Hey Kenny, what's happening?" Mae greeted the brother in the middle. "I want to introduce you to my dude I told you about earlier this morning. He's my man and he's cool to deal with."

Kenny reached out and gave Malik daps. "Whuz up, what you need?" Kenny said.

"I'm cool for right now, but this weekend I'm gonna need to re-up," Malik replied.

"You're good, let me know when. My number's 883-2216," Kenny said. "Let me have yours."

"482-5611." Malik gave him the number that the police could listen in on. He then turned to Mae. "Thanks baby girl, I can take it from here. Don't you have to hit them books and study?"

"You right about that," Mae said. "I'll catch up with you later," she said then strolled back down the hall and down the stairs.

"So, you brothas get down on the basketball court?" Malik asked Kenny and the others.

"Yeah, we hit the court every once in a while. Why, do you ball?" Kenny asked.

"I got some game. Maybe sometime we can relax and play a little," Malik said.

"You got it brotha. In the meantime, I'll wait for that call."

"You got it." Malik held up his balled fist and this time gave Kenny dabs. "I'm out brothas." Malik headed back down the stairs and out of the apartment building.

As he drove out of the complex, he knew he was in. From this point on it would be pretty easy to set Kenny up for the fall. But in doing so, he was putting Mae in harm's way. There was a strong possibility that she would end up going to jail for just making the introduction. She would also be in harm's way with Kenny if he found out it was Malik who would set him up. That could definitely mean her life. But unfortunately, that was the game; take advantage of those who don't know any better and use them to get to key players. It had been so easy for him to get to Mae and use her and he didn't really know her that well.

The next day Malik went in early in order to brief Lieutenant Bronson and Ms. Laura Chante from the Attorney General's office. They met in the Lieutenant's office.

"I've pretty much made contact with Kenny Holloway." Malik sat across from Bronson and Chante at the conference table in the Lieutenant's office. They both had yellow legal pads and pens ready to jot down pertinent information from him. "I'll set up the direct buy from Kenny within the next few days. Yesterday I told him I was okay, but would need to re-up by the end of the week."

"He talked sells with you and he just met you?" Bronson asked.

"Yeah, only because Mae brought me to him. They've lived in those projects all their lives. In fact, they've been friends since elementary school. He trusts her and knows she wouldn't deliberately set him up for a bust."

"Well, that's exactly what she's done," Chante said while writing notes on the legal pad.

"Not really," Malik shot back. "I mean she hasn't deliberately betrayed their friendship."

"Well, she should've busted him a long time ago if she knew he was dealing drugs," Bronson added.

"Hey come on, Lieutenant, let's be fair. They're friendship is deeper than what he does for a living. They grew up together and even though she knows what he does is wrong, they're still friends."

"He's a drug dealer," Bronson's voice rose. "He's poisoning the neighborhood, killing kids and anyone else who gets hooked on that junk. What do you mean she shouldn't have blown the whistle on him? She's an enabler and all those people living in those projects are enablers to a crime 'cause they know what's going on and won't report it, and when asked they tell us they just don't know nothing."

"Maybe that's because they dislike us more than the dealers and what they're doing," Malik shot back at the lieutenant.

"Okay, okay, let's not fight over this," Chante intervened. "We got fish to fry and need to decide when it's going down."

"This weekend," Malik said. "I'll make the buy on Saturday, then with the warrant ready, we can go in that night."

"Kenny is the biggest dealer in Dupont. We bust him and we'll put a real dent in that operation for a while," Bronson said.

"I doubt that, but at least it will be a start," Malik demurred. "Chante, I want to ask a favor that we not arrest Mae. She—"

"What," Bronson scowled. "She's got to go down too if she's conspiring to the selling of drugs. She knows better and she knows it's a crime. She has to go to jail just like the rest of them."

"That's not necessarily so." Malik allowed a little pleading in his voice. "She only did it because she's attracted to me. She only knows these guys because of a forced living environment that she had no control over. This is not something she usually does."

"That's a bunch of crap," Bronson shouted. "I'm so sick and tired of these tired old excuses for that criminal element. The whole idea that she's just a victim of her circumstances doesn't fly with me. She's a criminal and should be treated like one."

"She really doesn't think she's doing anything wrong." Malik refused to back off.

"Does she know you want to buy drugs?" Bronson asked, this time in a lower voice.

"Yes," Malik answered. "I guess it's hard for you to understand unless you grew up in that kind of environment. I did and I understand how she could get caught up in it and not really be a part of it." He knew he was making no progress with Bronson so he turned his attention to Chante. "I'm asking for special consideration in this case."

"Malik has greater knowledge of the particulars because he's the one working the case," Chante said. "He knows what's going on and who the key players are. I think we should accept his recommendation."

"I can't believe this." Bronson abruptly stood up. "I need some air." He rushed out of his office and left Malik and Chante sitting at the table.

"He'll be all right," Chante said. "Give him a few minutes to cool off."

Malik wasn't concerned with Bronson. His entire concentration was to make sure that Mae didn't have to do any time. He wasn't sure how he would be able to live with himself if that happened.

"I need to be taken into custody and locked up with Kenny and his boys," he said.

"We can do that."

"And you just got to be careful and keep Mae's identity with me quiet."

"The only way to do that is if Kenny pleads. If the case doesn't go to trial then we won't have to bring you in to testify. That's the only way she won't be implicated." She stopped and put her notepad in the briefcase. "Given Kenny's past record he will probably want to work out a plea and given how crowded our dockets are that'll be what happens. He might end up being an informant."

"Not mine," Malik said emphatically as they made it back out into the general area. "Tomorrow's Friday and I'll call Kenny and set up the buy for Saturday morning."

"That'll work," Chante said. "Oh, and one more thing, Malik."

"Yeah what's that?"

"Don't forget who you're working with. Don't forget whose side you're on." Chante finished and walked away.

Malik was beginning to view this war on drugs as a contradiction. The true criminals get off by cutting deals and turning informant. Those that just happened to be in the wrong place and the wrong time and didn't know the rules of the game were the real victims. They were the ones being used in the game by both the police and the drug dealers. Malik thought the game was enormous and he didn't know if he was being played, and just one of the many pawns in the game. What was really clear, no one really wanted the drug game to end. The dealers thought they were winning by making money-selling drugs, but their cut amounted to pennies compared to the suppliers. Their major contribution to the total game was to destroy any normalcy in the Black community. They called crack "girl" for a reason. Black girls had a strong addiction to the drug to the point of abandoning their role in the Black family. Essentially you destroy the female and you have destroyed the foundation of the Black family. Even the police officers were being used with the poisoning of their minds about an entire community.

Malik didn't like the game, but knew there was nothing he could do about it at least not at that time. He vowed that when the opportunity presented itself, he was going to educate as many young minds as possible that the actions taken by them as socially acceptable within their peer group and community were against the law. He was sure that Mae never thought that she could get prison time for simply introducing him to Kenny. He knew education was the only way to make a difference. Some day he would proclaim loud and clear that it is all a game and we are being played.

****

"Kenny, whuz up, fam?" Malik used his cell phone from his apartment. It was Saturday morning and everything was ready for the bust.

"Whuz up with you, fam?" Kenny hollered back from the other end, also on a cell phone.

"I need to make that move."

"What you need?"

"I need a bird if the price is right."

"Twenty thousand," Kenny said.

"That'll work."

"Cool, give me a couple of hours, and call me back. I'll tell you where to meet me."

Malik hit the off button and then dialed Bronson's number at the station. The entire unit was on call for the bust.

"Lieutenant, it's a go," he said to Bronson on the other end.

"Good, I got people in place," Bronson replied. "We'll initiate the surveillance on Kenny."

"Don't blow it."

"We know what we're doing. You just take care of your part." Malik knew he was alluding to Mae. Under these circumstances, he couldn't dare go to her and tell her to leave the vicinity or go visit someone else. Even though he was quite sure she had no idea about the game, it might create some suspicion and cause her to warn Kenny. He had to bite his bottom lip and bare it.

Malik sat in the lieutenant's office at headquarters with Bronson and Ms. Chante listening to the report that had just come in from the surveillance team. "The prime target was spotted leaving his residence at 10 a.m. with three other men. They drove a dark-colored Lexus registered to the prime target's mother. They were followed to a row house at 120 West 34th Street in the city.

The four men entered the house and about fifteen minutes later two females exited the house, got in the Lexus, and drove off. One of the vehicles with the surveillance team stayed behind to monitor the prime target's movement; the other team followed the two females."

While he listened his thoughts still were with Mae. She got up that morning, probably began studying for her exams with no idea that her entire life would be turned upside down if they arrested her. She could possibly do jail time and her dream of escaping the projects and building a better life for her daughter as well as herself would go up in smoke. And Malik would only have himself to blame. The surveillance team continued.

"The two females drove to an upscale part of town and parked in a cul-de-sac. They entered the residence at 4802 Big Rock Circle. They stayed in there only a short while and exited with four black duffel type bags. They drove back to the residence at 120 West 34th Street. The females were met by the prime target and the other men standing outside waiting for them. The prime target took the duffel bags back into the residence at 120 West 34th Street. Shortly thereafter, the prime target and the three men got back into the Lexus without the duffel bags and went back to the apartment in Dupont Projects. Surveillance teams were stationed at 4802 Big Rock Circle and 120 West 34th Street. Surveillance teams observed three other vehicles coming to 4802 Big Rock Circle and the same activity took place with females loading duffel bags from the residence to the trunk of their vehicles and driving to different locations in the city."

"Add those addresses to the warrant list," Bronson said to one of the police officers in the room with them.

At 2:00 p.m. Malik received the call.

"Hey, fam, come on over to the projects and meet me in the courtyard," Kenny instructed. He sounded all businesslike in his tone.

"No problem," Malik said. He turned to Bronson. "That's it. He's yours now."

"No, he's ours," Bronson corrected Malik.

"What about the girl?"

"Don't know. We might let her alone."

Malik and two other undercover detectives, who took the names of Dre and Devonte, left headquarters and headed for the place where the buy would take place. As he pulled off in the Maxima, Malik felt just a little nervous about Bronson's agreeing to leave Mae alone. It really didn't sound sincere.

Malik, Devonte, and Dre pulled into the projects where they spotted Kenny and his boys waiting in the courtyard. Malik backed the Maxima up next to Kenny's Lexus. They all three got out and walked over next to Kenny.

"These my cousins. They cool. I told you about them yesterday," Malik said as he greeted Kenny with the playa grip.

Kenny stared at Devonte and Dre for a minute then smiled and said, "Come on back here with me."

Malik followed him to the back of the car and Kenny popped the trunk. He grabbed a small duffel bag. "A brick," he said.

Malik opened the bag and checked out a solid brick of cocaine. He then strolled back over to his Maxima, popped the trunk, and pulled out a briefcase. He opened it and peeled off twenty thousand dollars in hundred-dollar bills.

Malik took the duffel bag and tossed it in the back of the Maxima. He and Kenny signaled to their boys that everything was cool. The two men gave each other the playa handshake and the three of them climbed back in the car.

"I'll be giving you a holla in a couple of days," Malik said and they drove out of the projects with the drugs.

Once out of the projects and off the main street, Malik pulled into a secure area where he pulled out a field test kit and checked the white substance. It tested positive for cocaine. Malik opened his cell phone and dialed Bronson's number.

"It tested positive so you can execute the warrants," he said.

The arrest went like clockwork. Two females were taken into custody at the West 34th Street residence and three kilos of cocaine were seized. Two males were arrested at Big Circle Drive along with ten kilos. An additional raid took place at 1520 131st Street, where four men were taken into custody and five kilos of cocaine were seized. Lieutenant Bronson and Agent Chante decided not to execute the warrant against Kenny and his boys at that same time, making it difficult to trace the bust to Malik and also implicate Mae. But it was coming.

Two days past and Malik had no contact with Mae. He just couldn't do that knowing that her turn might be coming soon. She called a couple of times, but he put her off, hoping she'd get angry and not call him anymore. On the fourth day, it was time to move on Kenny and his gang. He placed a call to Kenny monitored by Lieutenant Bronson and Chante.

"Whuz up, fam," Kenny said, answering Malik's call on the third ring.

"Trying to get a couple of birds if you got them?"

"Nah, it's too hot right now. One of my main connections got popped so I'm laying low. I got a bird I'm sittin' on and that's about it."

"Do what you gotta do fam till it cools off and hit me up when you ready," Malik said.

"Cool, I got some peeps I can turn you onto. Let me holla at them and I'll get back with you."

"For sure fam, I'll holla at you later." Malik finished and turned off the phone, stuck it in his pocket, and looked across the conference table at Bronson and Chante.

"I think we need to go after him now," Bronson said. "We don't want too much time to pass. Let's hit him while he's sitting on that one kilo."

"I agree," Chante said. "Since the warrant is in place, we need to execute it. He'll think the folks from the bust the other day gave him away and that'll keep you out of it, Malik."

"You going to leave the girl alone?" Malik asked.

Bronson and Chante looked at each other but said nothing.

"What's the deal?" Malik pursued the question.

"Just leave that alone right now," Bronson snapped at Malik. "You got a job to do. We'll be ready in the next hour."

Malik knew not to push the issue. He could only hope that Bronson and Chante would exercise some discretion and leave Mae alone. He turned and hurried out of the room.

Malik, Dre, and Devonte sat waiting in a sub-station five blocks from headquarters. That's where they would be arrested and brought back into the headquarters, but it had to be after Kenny and his gang were brought in for booking. It had to appear that the police made a clean sweep and arrested Malik also so that the dealers wouldn't be able to pinpoint him as the agent. They had also waited the extra days so that it would appear that one of the dealers arrested during the original bust had cut a deal with the police and gave Kenny and his crew up for a lighter sentence.

Malik paced the floor unable to calm his nerves. He wasn't concerned about the arrest, but about Mae. They told him that she might not go down with this bust, but what if she did? How would that affect her and if it was happening just then, how did she feel? He knew she would be frightened to the extent of panicking. But why was he so worried about her? She was there to be used and he did what was necessary. The person he should be thinking and worrying about was Jonetta. Since he started this new job with the department, they'd spent very little time together. Right after this bust, he promised himself that he'd take a break and spend some time with her. She deserved it because she'd been very patient and understanding with the lack of attention she'd gotten from him. It was all good with her and he had to make sure it stayed that way.

His cell phone went off and he came back to reality. "Yeah, this is Malik."

"It's done," Bronson practically shouted in the phone. "We got them all, you can come on in now."

"We'll be there in less than thirty," Malik said. "It's done, cuff us and take us in," he said to the police officers waiting with them.

Malik, Dre, and Devonte were cuffed, put in the back of a police wagon, and taken back to the station. Still in cuffs, the police marched them into the booking area. As they marched in, Malik stopped right in the middle of the room.

Mae was sitting on the bench along the wall with Kenny and four other young men. Her head was down and he could tell she was crying. She looked up at him and the expression on her face told the whole story.

"Why?" she shouted at him. "Why did you do this to me? I told you no drugs or none of that mess in my place and now they think I had something to do with all this drug stuff. Malik, you got to tell them I didn't have anything to do with it. You know what this is doing to my child, my mother, and now I won't be able to stay in school." She burst out crying and covered her face. "Why you do this to me? Why you wreck my life like this?"

"Shut up," Malik shouted at her. "Just shut up. They ain't got nothing on none of us. So just shut up." He moved over to the fingerprint station. Malik knew the worst reaction he could possibly have is to show any compassion for her. There was no way he could reveal any semblance of the real Malik because Kenny would pick it up and know he was the culprit. As long as he kept up the façade, he'd be all right and later could clear Mae. But it hurt to know that all the things she said to him were true, not for the reason she thought, but for a much more devious reason.

The sergeant on duty in the booking room pushed Malik up against the wall and said, "Get over there and shut up yourself." He pushed Malik over to the fingerprint station and took his prints. They then shoved him over to another station and took his picture. Through it all, he could hear Mae sobbing. God, if he could just go to her and let her know it would all be okay. If he could tell her he was undercover and would be able to clear her name and get her out of this mess. But there was no chance he could do that. It would mean his death and probably hers also. The time would come when he could make this all up to her, but then and there he had to play the game.

The sergeant grabbed him by the arm and took him out of the room. A couple of other officers brought Dre and Devonte out also. Bronson and Chante waited for him on the other side of the station. He rushed Bronson and got right in his face.

"Why'd you arrest her? Why'd you go against your word?"

"We had to and you know it, even if we don't want to charge her. It had to look like we were after her also or her life wouldn't be worth two cents if Kenny thought she was involved in his bust. We'll charge her and get it reduced to a lower offense then let her go."

Malik backed off Bronson and sat in a chair to relax. He didn't know what to say to either Bronson or Chante, so instead, he just stared at the floor.

"Malik, great bust, man," the policeman who arrested and brought him into the station said as he passed by where Malik had sat down.

"Congratulations, man, you're on your way to a great career. You're a natural for this work," another officer said.

"Detective Malik Williams, you are an outstanding officer, and I'd like to recommend you to the DEA," Chante said. "We need more Black undercover agents to penetrate your communities. Sometimes it's very difficult for the white agent. You have a knack with young Black dealers and they'll trust you. That's what we need. Great job," She finished and walked away.

Malik didn't look up while receiving accolades from his fellow officers or when Chante suggested that he go to work for the Feds in undercover. He didn't acknowledge their compliments. He didn't feel good about himself. All along he thought he might make a difference being undercover and putting dealers in jail. Bottom line was that young brothers like Kenny didn't go to jail. They cut deals with the District Attorney and often got off on probation. They knew the system and understood every step of the way what they were doing. The Kennys of the Black community calculated their risks against the kind of lifestyle dealing drugs would provide them and they were willing to take a chance. But people like Mae didn't understand nor did they want to be in the game. They were the ones that often got trapped and their lives destroyed. Our communities may be home sweet home to most of our people, he thought, but in reality, it's just a playground for drug dealers and cops. Malik couldn't do this anymore. He gave it a shot, but it hurt more than it made him feel good. He had to stay true to himself and not get caught up in this vicious game. He had locked up a drug dealer, but practically shattered Mae's life in the process.

He got up and slowly walked to the detective's locker room, all the time fighting back the tears. He looked in the mirror and no longer saw that man who, not long ago, told Jonetta that this work would be for only a short time and that his heart was still set on community service. He had to make that happen and real soon. There was no way he could spend one more day as an undercover agent, giving him no fulfillment. In order to believe in himself, he had to rediscover the love for himself. That could never happen doing work that ultimately would have the opposite effect.

He opened his locker and tore off the dreadlocks. Malik stripped down to his waist, strolled over to the washbasin, and threw water all over his exposed body. He needed to wash away the filth, like cleansing his soul and purging it of the sordid kind of business he was now tied up in. He changed clothes and hurried out of that place, maybe for the last time. It now depended on whether the higher-ups would make the transfer he knew must happen.

Friday Night Wagon Wheel

Antoinette Winstead

"Here you go, Alexandra."

"Thank you, ma'am."

"What did I say about calling me ma'am?"

"I'm sorry, ma—I mean, Allison." Alex took the beveled iced tea glass from the long graceful fingers of Allison Sinclair-George and smiled up at possibly the most beautiful woman she'd even seen in person.

Allison Sinclair-George had a flawless, Photoshop-esque, milk chocolate complexion; short cropped, natural hair, ala Lupita Nyong'o; large almond-shaped brown eyes, surrounded by impossibly long thick black lashes; and a ballerina's lithe, lean physique—beautifully accentuated in the sleeveless, butter-yellow summer dress she wore. Realizing that she probably looked like a grinning idiot, Alex tried to suppress her smile. But, she couldn't help it. This was *the* Allison Sinclair-George, International Human Rights lawyer extraordinaire, whose name made human rights violators quake in their bloodied boots and here she was serving her, Alexandra "Alex" Stevens, sweet ice tea when only last month this courtroom diva had been in the Hague serving up heads on ubiquitous silver trays.

"She's only doing what she's been taught, to respect her elders," Dr. Benjamin George, wearing khaki pants and a blue polo, chimed in from a burgundy leather armchair, flanking the stone-hearth fireplace. He was a tall, trim, handsome silver-haired man in his mid-eighties, his cinnamon brown skin flawed only by a web of smile lines radiating out from his large, dark-brown eyes, hidden behind a pair of rimless glasses. "And if you ask me," Benjamin continued, "there's not enough of it these days."

"Not enough what?" Brandon George asked, striding through the double sliding doors of Benjamin's cozy, private library in tan cargo pants and a red polo. He was a younger version of his grandfather, only handsomer and taller, with laughing, mischievous brown-eyes, full deliciously kissable lips—Alex mooned wistfully— and a well-honed physique, thanks to three days a week with a private trainer, which Alex had read about in *Jet Magazine*. Being in a room with these three was like being in the midst of a supermodel photo shoot for *Vanity Fair*, Alex thought, feeling suddenly self-conscious and, more than a little, inadequate in her well-worn cowboy boots, faded jeans, and pink cotton print blouse. Had she known she'd be interviewing the likes of the George's this summer, she would have packed a suit or at least a nice dress.

"Respect," Allison interjected and handed Benjamin one of the three remaining tea glasses on the silver service tray.

Standing behind his grandfather's chair, Brandon said, with a sly grin and wink to his wife, "Oh that."

Allison rolled her eyes at her husband's playful antics and handed him a glass of tea.

"Yes, *that*," Benjamin tossed over his shoulder. "You two could learn a thing or two from this young lady. Raised right, I say." Benjamin tilted his glass toward Alex. "You just keep on with your, ma'am and sir, shows good breeding. 'Sides these two are too old to be called anything but."

Brandon snickered. "Speak for yourself, old man."

"Ain't too old for a switch, boy."

"You just said I was too old—"

"You sassin' me, son?"

"Alright, you two, back to your corners," Allison sat the serving tray on the mahogany coffee table in front of the brown leather sofa where Alex sat, mesmerized by the playful exchange between, unequivocally, Freedom, Texas' royal family. "Alexandra didn't come out here to hear you boys bicker." Allison took a seat next to Alex on the sofa and crossed her elegant brown legs at the ankle. "Did you?" Alex felt her lips stretch into another obscenely wide idiotic grin. Allison gave her jean-clad knee a sympathetic pat. "It's alright. They always get a bit feisty before nap time."

"If you're implying," Benjamin said, "that our behavior is childlike—"

"Who's implying," Allison interjected.

"In that case—"

"What?" Ann Louise George, short and petite, breezed into the room, her silver hair swept back into a thick bun at the nape of her slender, coffee brown neck where a gold necklace with a sapphire pendant hung, matching the summer blouse and pedal pushers she wore. Alex prayed that if she ever lived to see eighty that she looked half as good as Miss Ann Louise did at age eighty-three. "You'll sue your own wife? Be a waste of money, because, my dear grandson, you would lose."

Brandon pouted. "You're taking her side over your own flesh and blood?"

"There, there." Ann Louise patted Bandon's cheek. "Hasn't anyone ever told you that gender is thicker than blood?"

"Humph, learn something new every day," Benjamin said, taking a sip of his tea.

"That's right," Ann Louise said. "And as long as you're learning, you know you're not dead."

Allison raised her glass, "Here! Here!" then sipped.

"Well now that we're all warmed up," Ann Louise said as she crossed the room to the Queen Ann armchair at the end of the coffee table nearest to Alex and sat down on the crimson brocade cushion, "shall we begin and stop wasting this young lady's time?"

Waste away, Alex thought, soaking in the pleasure of being surrounded by medical and political celebrity.

Until today, she'd been utterly miserable. Interning at her grandfather's small-town newspaper for the summer didn't figure into the greatest moments of her life. In fact, she'd listened with envy as her classmates bragged about their summer internships. A couple of students were going to New York City, another to D.C., even her roommate had landed one in London. But where was she going, Freedom, Texas to work at the *Freedom Gazette*. Woohoo! Stop the presses!

Yes, she had to admit she'd had a couple of unexpectedly interesting interviews, but this...this was the kind of access that reporters at *The Post* and *The Times* hadn't been granted. And here she was, not only sitting in the private library of Dr. Benjamin George—a room lined with dark oak wood bookshelves, housing the first editions of books authored by not only him, but also his wife, son, grandson, and granddaughter-in-law— but actually sitting across the room from the man himself, the famed Howard University graduate, and his wife, Dr. Ann Louise George, Meharry University graduate, who just happened to be the grandparents of Brandon Jefferson George, U.S. Congressman, pegged to be the next African-American president—if Cory Booker didn't beat him to it— and his wife, Allison Sinclair-George. When word got out that she'd snagged this interview, she would be the envy of every student in her UT Journalism program. It might even bolster up her portfolio enough to get her into Columbia University's Graduate School of Journalism—her dream program—along with about a million other undergrads around the world. But, she was jumping ahead. She had to get the interview first.

"So, child, what would you like to know?" Benjamin asked.

Everything, she wanted to say, but instead said, "Thank you for allowing me to interview you today."

"Our pleasure, dear," Ann Louise said. "Your grandfather is like family to us."

"He was one of the first babies I delivered. You remember, Lou-Lou?"

"Yes I was in my last year at Meharry and you called me in the middle of the night, all out of breath and excited like a little boy on Christmas day. 'Lou-Lou, it's a boy! It's a boy!' You sounded like a drunken fool— a lovable drunken fool."

"That's how I won her over," Benjamin said proudly.

"If you say so, dear," Ann Louise said primly. "But I don't think Alexandra's here to hear our love story. I believe her interest lies in more relevant events involving, for instance, my handsome grandson and his beautiful wife."

"Is that right, Alexandra? You're more interested in him," he gestured his head toward Brandon, "than me?"

"Don't embarrass yourself, Pops," Brandon said, "you know she is."

"See, this is how they treat you once you get old. Take my advice, Alexandra, don't get old or at least don't have any ungrateful grandchildren."

"Ah, Pops, you know I appreciate all you've ever done for me." Brandon leaned over the back of his grandfather's chair and gave Benjamin a big bear hug and kiss on the cheek.

Benjamin playfully pushed him away. "Now who's embarrassing himself? Show a little dignity, son.

We've got company."

"Right, Pops!" Brandon patted Benjamin's thin shoulders then crossed to the matching burgundy leather armchair flanking the opposite side of the fireplace and sat down. "So, Alexandra, fire away."

"Okay," Alex said. "Do you mind if I record this?"

"Fine with me," Brandon said. "Okay with everyone else?"

The others nodded in agreement.

"Thank you." Alex turned on her digital recorder and flipped open her notepad to the first page and the list of ten questions she'd spent all night preparing. She took a deep breath to steady her nerves then asked the first question, "Congressman George, you come from two generations of notable doctors—both your paternal grandparents and your father—what made you chose law and politics over a profession in medicine?"

"Good question," Brandon said then settled back in his chair to consider his answer. "I thought about medicine," he said after a moment, "but I didn't feel it in here." He tapped his chest above his heart. "If you're going to devote your time and energy to something that you plan to spend the rest of your life doing, you've got to feel it. It has to be the air you breathe. The things you wake up and go to sleep thinking about. It's like being in love." He glanced at Allison and smiled. "And I didn't feel that way about medicine. I respect the profession and admire my grandparents and father for all they've done to further healthcare in the African- American community, but I was gifted with a legal mind. My talent, if you will, lies in helping people with their legal issues. And as time has passed, I've found the best way to make a difference and to help people is through politics and trying to ensure that the Constitution works for everyone, not just the privileged few. And before you ask," Brandon said anticipating what Alex might ask as a follow-up to his last statement, "I am one of the privileged few, but it doesn't mean I've had it easy. Very few Africa American men can claim they've had it easy, no matter what their economic status or pedigree."

"Amen to that," Benjamin said.

"Now, I won't pretend that I've had it anywhere near as hard as my grandfather or father, but I've had my share of run-ins."

"May I ask what kind?"

"Well, there's always D.W.B." Alex eyed him quizzically. "Driving while black," Brandon said. Alex nodded and made a quick note in her pad.

"In my day," Benjamin chimed in, "it was walking while black."

'This is Brandon's interview, dear," Ann Louise said.

"It's alright, Grandma, I think Alexandra might be interested in this one." Brandon turned to Benjamin. "Tell Alexandra about the Friday night wagon wheels."

"Oh, now, son," Benjamin said with a wave of his hand, "she didn't come here to hear my old stories." He feigned modesty garnered snickers from his family, well acquainted with his games.

"We won't force you, Pops," Brandon said with a subtle wink to his wife. "But, it is one of the primary reasons I decided to go into law. You see, Alexandra, when Pops was about twenty-one—"

"Now if you're going to tell it, tell it right," Benjamin interjected. "I was twenty-seven, going on twenty- eight back in 1955."

"Oh yeah, that's right, twenty-seven. And it was cold, blustery night in December—"

"Confounded it, son." Agitated, Benjamin uncrossed his legs and leaned forward. "No wonder you people never get anything accomplished up there in Washington, can't keep your facts straight."

"But you said, Alexandra didn't come to hear you, and it is the story that changed my life. So, I think I should—"

"Let someone who knows it, tell it," Benjamin interrupted. "The direction you're headed, they'll be some kind of alien abduction next."

Brandon held up his hands in surrender. "Alright, it's your story."

Knowing looks passed between Brandon, Allison, and Ann Louise, as Brandon settled back in his chair, re-crossed his legs and made himself comfortable.

All sorted, Benjamin nodded to Alex, "Alexandra did your grandfather ever tell you about the Friday night wagon wheel?"

"No, sir."

"Umm, not too surprising. It's not really the kind of story for a youngster's ears."

Brandon guffawed. "You had no trouble telling me when I was, how old? Eight? Nine?"

"You were a precocious child, too old for your years, and full of mischief," Benjamin said.

"Could have traumatized me," Brandon protested with devilish pout.

Benjamin waved him off and said, "A boy who wanted to wrangle rattlesnakes for a living? I don't think so."

Ann Louise leaned over to Alex to explain. "When Brandon was a boy, he wanted to wrangle rattlesnakes. He got the idea from one of those nature shows. So early one morning, before dawn, he takes one of my good pillow cases and the fireplace tongs, then proceeds to go hunting for rattlesnakes."

"Bagged three of them before breakfast," Brandon said proudly.

"I was standing at the stove—never forget it—scrambling eggs," Ann Louise said.

"In that pink chenille robe, I bought you for Christmas," Benjamin said, and then under his breath added coyly, "Always liked you in pink."

"Anyway," Ann Louise continued, unperturbed by her husband's interjection, "Ben was at the table reading the morning paper, and in strolls Brandon, tongs in one hand, gripping the opening of the pillowcase—all dirty and bulging—closed with the other. 'What you doing with my good pillowcase?' I asked. 'Wrangling snakes,' he said with a big toothless grin. Then he opened the bag and showed me." Ann Louise covered her heart with her hand, as if she could still feel it thundering in her chest from the shock. "Almost sent me to an early grave, seeing those things slithering around in there."

"They were alive?" Alex asked horrified.

"Yep, sure were," Brandon said proudly. "One was a five-footer too."

Allison shook her head. "Every time he tells it, I swear that snake gains another foot."

"Tall tales run in his family," Ann Louise added. "But he did have three, about a foot and a half each. Baby ones, which are, of course, the most poisonous."

Brandon puffed out his chest. "That's right—the most poisonous." He thumbed invisible suspenders and grinned.

Allison clasped her hands together and fluttered her eyelashes. "My hero."

"It was a twenty-four/seven job trying to keep him alive that summer," Ann Louise said with a fond glint in her eye; although, Alex doubted Ann Louis felt that way at the time. "Remember Ben?"

"He was a handful." Benjamin chuckled. "Thought for sure we were going to be shipping him back to his parents in a wooden box." Benjamin sighed, suddenly quite serious. "But those snakes were nothing compared to the night Brandon went missing."

A hush fell over the room that sent a small ripple of fearful anticipation down Alex's spine. She could hear the faint chirping of birds; the rhythmic singing of cicadas; and the rustle of leaves in the gentle summer breeze, coming from the well-tended garden, beyond the heavily draped French doors of the library, which only served to heighten her unease, as those around her seemed to fall into a nostalgic trance, seeing and hearing things beyond the room, and time, in which they currently sat.

"Yes," Ann Louise said softly, breaking the silence, "that was an awful night."

"Sorry," Benjamin said, seeming to shrink into the armchair as if once again that small, precocious child of nine. "I had no idea at the time."

"Nor should you have," Ann Louise said. "You were just a boy being a boy."

"You're never just a boy being a boy when your skin is black," Benjamin admonished with a sad shake of his head. "But Brandon didn't know that. Hadn't been taught—"

"I think I'll get some more tea," Ann Louise said abruptly and pushed up from her chair, "Anyone else?

Alexandra?"

"No, ma'am, I'm fine."

Ann Louise nodded then crossed to the double doors, stopping briefly to place a soft kiss on the top of Brandon's head before continuing out of the room, her gait, Alex noted, not exactly steady. From the concern on the faces of the others, she guessed she was not the only one to notice.

"Allison, would you mind?" Benjamin said quietly after Ann Louise left.

"No, not at all." Allison smiled at Alex and patted her hand. "Not to worry, she'll be fine. She just doesn't care for this particular story. And, frankly, neither do I. But it's one that needs to be told and never forgotten. Because—"

"Forgetting leads to complacency," Brandon said, finishing her sentence. "Which, my beautiful wife fights against every day."

"That I do," Allison said, rising to her feet.

"And quite successfully, I might add," Brandon said, beaming like the proud husband he obviously was.

"Why thank you, kind sir." Allison dipped her head in deference to her husband's compliment.

"Not at all, my dear." They exchanged an intimate smile then Allison strode gracefully out of the room, Brandon's eyes never wavering from her until she turned down the hall.

Alex felt a slight pang of envy, watching Brandon watch Allison, wondering what it must be like to be loved as much as it seemed he loved her, and she loved him. But then, she thought, trying to dampen the green-eyed monster threatening to invade, no relationship was perfect. Although, she'd bet a million dollars that their imperfect was loads better than most people's.

"Now that the women folk have fled—"

"Pops!" Brandon gasped. "Please forgive him, Alexandra. His generation isn't exactly PC."

"Meaning I call a spade a spade, my dear, which is why I could never be a politician, like my grandson, here. Too much of that double-speak and dodging about, never directly answering a question."

Alex recognized this playful banter for what it was, avoidance, but she wasn't exactly sure how to steer this particular conversation back to the story that had so effectively cleared the room of the so called, "women folk," of which she seemed excluded, despite her gender. She didn't want to be rude, but any story that could cause Allison Sinclair-George to leave a room, was one that she definitely wanted to hear, and preferably before she turned eighty, so she took a deep steadying breath and said quietly, "Dr. George, you were saying that the snakes were nothing compared to the night that Congressman George went missing. Why is that?"

Benjamin and Brandon exchanged knowing looks then Benjamin gestured to Alex with his head, "Just like her grandfather, on point, not distracted by the sideshow." Benjamin then directed his attention to her and said, "You're going to make a mighty fine reporter, young lady."

After a couple more playful exchanges and jabs, Benjamin finally settled in to tell his story. Alex pointed her digital recorder in his direction and, with her pencil poised to capture any nuisance or gesture beyond the recorder's capabilities, waited for him to begin.

Benjamin took a long sip of tea, cleared his throat, then said, 'The summer Brandon decided to try his hand at snake wrangling was also the summer he decided to pull a Huck Finn—"

"Beg your pardon, Pops," Benjamin interrupted, "but it was the Hardy Boys." He leaned forward and said to Alex, "My mom had bought me the first ten books in the series the winter before and I was hooked. And, what better place to emulate my newfound heroes than Freedom, Texas? I was absolutely convinced that there had to be some old silver mine and haunted house in the area, so late one night," he paused and looked at Benjamin. "You don't mind if I tell this part, do you?"

Benjamin waved his hand. "Go right ahead. It's yours to tell."

"So I was saying, late one night after everyone had gone to bed, I packed my backpack with the essentials I knew I'd need for my adventure—flashlight, BB gun, rope, canteen of water, a box of Pop Tarts, and my favorite *Captain America* comic. I tiptoed past Pops and Grandma's bedroom, down the backstairs to the kitchen, snuck out the backdoor and headed for the woods. Had no idea where I was going, only that I was headed for an adventure."

"His little adventure," Benjamin chimed in, "had the entire town up and searching for his bad butt all night and into the early hours of the morning." He sighed heavily. "Thought for sure we'd find you laid up dead some place, or worse."

"Sorry, Pops." Brandon reached over and laid his hand on the older man's bony knee. "I didn't know."

"No reason you should have. I mean, a boy should be able to go out and have himself a little adventure without fearing for his life. But that's just not how things were then or, if Jasper is any indication, are now." Benjamin fell silent for a moment, seeming to gather his thoughts.

"A doctor sees things most people never will," he said finally. "Some amazing, like the birth of a baby. Others pretty horrific, like the damage a telephone pole can do a young girl's body. I've seen some of everything, but the thing that stands out the most, the thing that had me frantic the night Brandon went missing, was what I saw nearly sixty years ago, back in 1955 when I was a young man of twenty-seven. Now, I wasn't naive by any stretch of the imagination, but this...this was beyond anything I'd ever heard about or seen. And believe me, growing up in Texas, with its infamous monthly lynchings advertised in city newspapers around the state like Sunday socials, you'd think there's nothing that can ever beat that, but..." He paused, considering the insanity of it all, and shook his head. "I guess between the Klan and the Nazi's nothing should be beyond the imagination when it comes to how cruel one human can be to another."

His words conjured in Alex's mind images of burning crosses, burnt bodies hanging from trees, people being herded into boxcars, and piles of emaciated corpses being bulldozed into giant pits. She shivered slightly and gripped her pencil tighter, not wanting to betray her revulsion, for fear Benjamin would mistake it for female weakness and refuse to tell her his story.

"I was driving home after a long day over at Shelby General where I was interning. They had a colored ward back then and I shared an office with the only other black doctor in the county, Dr. Elijah Jones. He must have been close to eighty then, but still going strong."

"Just like you, Pops," Brandon said.

Benjamin chuckled. "At my age, I doubt they'd let me anywhere near a surgery these days, but Dr. Jones...he was still operating and with a steady hand well into his early nineties. The only thing that stopped him was a massive heart attack that sent him directly to his grave. I loved that old man; taught me more in one year about life and medicine than I ever learned in medical school, but that's off the record, young lady."

"Yeah," Brandon said, "he wouldn't want his alma mater removing his name from that fancy bronze plaque they just installed in his honor."

"As much money as I've given it should be a statue. But again, that's off the record." He winked at Alex. "Wouldn't want to stir up the hornets unnecessarily."

"Yes, sir." She made a note to herself on the pad and said, "Done. Off the record."

"Good. Now," Benjamin continued, "it was a Friday night and I was dog-tired, looking forward to sleeping for the next twenty-four hours. For some reason, I decided to take the old Miller Road. Back then it was a couple dozen miles of woods on either side of what amounted to a two-lane gravel tract. But it was a pleasant drive and just what I needed to clear my head.

"It was late June, a little after eleven p.m., but still stifling hot and I had my window down, trying to catch a breeze. I remember how the dust from the road swirled in the headlights of my black Chevy and how all I could think about was getting home to take a long hot bath, and to curl up in bed next to my beautiful bride," he said with a sly grin. "I must have been daydreaming about that bath—"

"Yeah, the *bath*," Brandon said facetiously.

Benjamin held up two fingers. "That's two, son. One more and—"

"Got it, Pops." Brandon mimed buttoning his lips. "Continue, please."

"Anyway, I was daydreaming, not really paying any mind to what was ahead of me when suddenly this bloodied, naked black man runs out in the road in front of the car. And just like a deer, he freezes in the beam of the headlights. I swerved to miss him and nearly drove off the road into the ditch. I slammed on my brakes and craned around, expecting to see a body lying in the road. But there he was, still standing there, a dark silhouette in the moonlight, frozen in place like a Greek statue with his arms akimbo.

"I jumped out of the car and jogged back to where he stood. Now, I'm not one to believe in the supernatural, but the closer I got the more other worldly the whole thing felt. I slowed down, a bit hesitant, and called out to him. 'Hey, you alright? Can I help you?' But he didn't move." Benjamin paused and looked past Alex, seeing beyond the room to the lonely, dark road and the man silhouetted in the moonlight. "I reached out and touched his shoulder and it was like an electronic charge passed between us, sparking him to life. He spun around, eyes bulging, feral with fear, ready to run-off; but, somehow, I managed to restrain him, hold him. He struggled against me and kept saying, 'Please don't hurt me no more. Please!' But in his weakened condition, he was no match for me. I had at least six inches and thirty pounds on him. After all, he was just a boy, tall for his age, but barely fourteen, I found out later.

"I assured him that I meant him no harm. And, after a while—don't know how long exactly—he calmed enough to let me lead him back to the car. I wrapped him in a flannel blanket I had in the trunk and settled him on the backseat. I needed to get him back to Shelby so I could assess his injuries, knowing that my long-awaited weekend off was not to be.

"I started the engine and was preparing to pull off when the young man sat up and shouted, 'No! Tommy Lee! We gotta get Tommy Lee.' I thought he was maybe delusional from the shock of whatever trauma he'd suffered and, once again, tried to calm him. But he was insistent that there was a Tommy Lee, who needed saving.

"'Alright,' I said, hoping that playing along would calm him down, 'where is he?'

"'Down by the river,' he said.

"Now keep in mind, it was well after midnight by now and the only other light beside my headlights was the full moon. And being the practical man I was, I had no desire to go traipsing through the woods down to the river to save someone I wasn't sure even existed. But I also understood that my new patient's agitation would not abate until I did as he wanted.

"To my pleasant surprise, he told me there was a dirt track leading to the river, wide enough for my car to drive down. He directed me to the track and we bumped down it for about fifteen minutes, finally emerging from the dense foliage onto a thin strip of muddy beach.

"Had it been on another occasion, under different circumstances, one with Lou-Lou by my side, the embers from the smoldering camp fire and moonlight dancing off the rippling waters of the river, would have made this secreted spot perfect for a romantic interlude. Instead, it only served to highlight the horror of what awaited us on this pseudo beachfront.

"'Tommy Lee,' my patient whimpered from the backseat as he fumbled to open the backdoor.

"'Stay there!' I ordered and without thinking of my own possible danger, got out of the car and walked toward the dying campfire near the river's edge and the wagon wheel propped up against a bolder where a young boy—no older than ten—sat naked, his arms stretched wide to either side of him and tied at the wrists to the spokes of the wheel with thick rope. His head hung limp, chin resting on his chest, which was bloodied and marred by what I later would learn were knife wounds from his captors who had used him for target practice. But not until after sodomizing him repeatedly and then cutting off his genitals, which they'd left nailed to the wagon wheel above his head."

Benjamin paused, took a deep breath, and exhaled. "You think you've seen the worst of what man has to offer, then...ten years old...that's all...To die like that because some good ole boys were bored on a Friday night and decided it might be fun to round up some black boys and use them for target practice..." Benjamin fell silent, the distant look in his eyes gradually dissipating.

Alex waited for him to return to the present before asking, "Did they catch them?" Benjamin eyed her quizzically. "The men, who did it, did they catch them?" she asked again.

Benjamin laughed sardonically. "Back in 1955, there was no such thing as catching a white man for doing any wrong against someone black. You'd have more luck catching a unicorn and flying off on a magic carpet. But everyone knew who did it. It was the Butler and Richmond boys. They went around town bragging to anyone who would listen about how many bull's eyes they scored, and how the 'little nigga had begged and cried for his daddy like a squealing pig.'"

"Oh my God," Alex shrieked with a shudder of disbelief. "And everyone knew?"

"That's just how things were back then."

Alex took a moment to let it sink in before asking, "What happened to the other one, the one who ran out in the street?"

"After I collected Tommy Lee's body, I drove Samuel—that was the other boy's name—back to Shelby General. He'd been beat-up and sodomized too and been told to wait his turn at the wheel. Lucky for him, they'd lost interest and that's how he'd managed to get away."

"And they weren't afraid he'd tell?" Alex asked trying to process the injustice and horror of what Samuel and Tommy Lee had experienced, all because they were black and violators knew they could get away with it because of the privilege their white skin afforded them.

"No, they weren't," Benjamin confirmed. "I did what I could to patch up his wounds, but God knows there was nothing I could do for his spirit. A couple days later, Samuel and his family packed up and moved to St. Louis—safer there than here. I heard— through the Freedom grapevine—that Samuel committed suicide a few years later."

"How awful," Alex whispered then lowered her head and pretended to make a note while she attempted to blink back the tears in her eyes. After all, what kind of reporter was she if she let her emotions get the better of her? She took a deep breath to steady her nerves then glanced back up at Benjamin. "And Tommy Lee's family?"

"They buried Tommy Lee and then a few weeks later moved to Pittsburgh."

Saddened, Alex shook her head. "And no one was ever prosecuted?"

"No. By the time the courts started reopening cold cases like this, that were obvious civil rights violations— when was it, Brandon, the late eighties? Early nineties?"

"Yeah, somewhere around then," Brandon said.

"Well by that time, the only witnesses were dead. Samuel, suicide, and the Butler and Richmond boys, killed in Nam—only good thing that come out of that war."

"Pops!" Brandon said.

"Okay, okay! Let's just keep that off the record too, alright, Alexandra?"

Alex nodded, although, she agreed wholeheartedly with Dr. George, and political correctness aside, doubted that anyone else would object to his sentiments.

Alex glanced over her notes, considered what Benjamin had told her, then said, "And this is why you were so frantic when Congressman George went missing? But weren't the Butler and Richmond boys dead by then?"

"They were, but not their legacy," Benjamin said.

Astonished, Alex gasped. "You mean this happened again?"

"At least a half-dozen more times, probably more, I suspect, but I only know about the ones here in Jamerson County. Got to the point, if you were a black male, you didn't dare go outside after six o'clock on a Friday night for fear of the wagon wheel."

"And you thought..." Alex said, trailing off as she put all the pieces together.

"Exactly." Benjamin glanced over at his grandson. "Brandon was the right age, ripe for target practice."

"You must have gone crazy," Alex said.

"Damn near—oh, excuse me, dear," Benjamin said, apologizing for his profanity. "We searched high and low for Brandon. Come sunrise, me and a couple of my close friends got our shotguns and headed over to Shelby, certain we'd find his body tied to a wagon wheel on that riverbank. That was the longest drive of my life. I'll never forget what it was like driving down that old dirt track, the sun coming up over the horizon, nearly blinding us as we drove onto the beach. Took a few seconds for my eyes to adjust; but when they did, I thought for sure I'd see him there, just like Tommy Lee..."

"But you didn't," Alex said softly.

"No, ma'am, I didn't." Benjamin glanced over at Brandon. "Thank God."

Alex could feel the enormity of his relief, even after all these years and considering what he'd witnessed with Tommy Lee and Samuel, she understood how such a powerful emotion could linger this long after the fact.

"We drove back here, relieved, but still worried half to death, as you can imagine, walked in through the backdoor and there he was, at the kitchen table, big as you please, eating a stack of blueberry pancakes and asking for more bacon, which Lou-Lou was frying up in her big cast iron skillet as if nothing was amiss. Half the town out looking for him and here he was, eating pancakes and bacon and jabbering on about his overnight sleep-out in some barn. I can't exactly remember what happened after that."

"How convenient, the 'I don't recall' defense," Brandon said. Benjamin waved him off. "The boy claims I spanked him."

"In today's parlance," Bandon said, "it would be classified as a beating, and a clear case of child abuse."

"Whatever you want to call it, it was well-deserved, and that you can't argue with your fancy legalese."

Brandon held up his hands in surrender, which Alex gathered was a familiar stance for him when it came to his grandfather. "You may have a point there, had tax dollars been used, but—"

"But nothing," Benjamin glared, daring Brandon to contradict him, then after a tense second, suddenly smiled and laughed heartedly. "You couldn't sit for a week as I recall—after my temporary backout that is."

"More like a month," Brandon chuckled.

"Never thought about going on another midnight adventure again, did you?"

"Nope!"

"Then I did my job."

"Is that when you told him about Tommy Lee and Samuel?" Alex asked.

"It was later that summer, after things calmed down a bit. It broke my heart to have to tell him, but truth is that at some point a young black boy must be introduced to the reality of the world he lives in. Besides, he was always mature for his age. Lou-Lou says he's got an old soul."

"And you told him everything?" Alex asked, imagining how frightening a story like that must have been for a young child, reality or not.

"I left out a few details—things I didn't think were suitable—like the sodomy and the genital mutilation."

"But what he did tell me," Brandon said, "made me want to fight the injustice of it all. Although at the time, I didn't have the language to describe it as such. As I said, it's the thing that made me want to be a lawyer. In fact, my first case was a civil rights case similar to what happened to Tommy Lee. It happened in the late sixties and all the alleged perps were still alive when it was reopened in 2001, old as dirt, but still alive. They're sitting on death row in Huntsville right now. It was my first big win, which, you could say, paved the way to where I am today."

"Any one for more tea?" Allison asked sweeping back into the room with a crystal pitcher of iced tea.

"Thank you, dear," Benjamin said, holding his glass aloft for her to fill.

"So how was the history lesson?" Allison said over her shoulder to Alex as she filled Benjamin's glass. "Hope it wasn't too distressing."

"Not at all," Alex lied. "Very informative."

"Good," Allison said, gliding over to her husband to refill his glass.

"I have fresh shortbread cookies," Ann Louise said, entering the room to join the gathering, in her hands a plate stacked with perfect circles of golden-brown cookies laced with pecan bits. "I got the recipe from a sweet little Highland's matron when we were Inverness forty odd years ago." She offered the plate to Alex, who took one. It was still warm to touch and the aroma of sugar and sweet butter instantly made her mouth water. "You can have more than one," Ann Louise tempted, but Alex demurred.

"Thank you, this is fine."

Ann Louise nodded and moved about the room, sharing her spoils with the rest of her family. "Lunch will be ready in a few minutes," Ann Louise said. "Would you care to join us, Alexandra? It's nothing fancy—ham, potato salad, corn bread and such."

Taken aback by the invitation, Alex stammered, "Oh, I couldn't impose."

Benjamin guffawed. "Not at all, child, these two eat like birds," he said gesturing to Brandon and Allison, "so there'll be plenty of food. Besides, you haven't finished your interview yet, have you?"

"Well..." Alex considered the proposal and what this bonus time could mean in regards to not only the article, but also her portfolio and said, "Thank you, I will."

Benjamin slapped his leg. "Wonderful. And I promise not to monopolize the conversation."

"Don't make promises you can't possibly keep, dear," Ann Louise admonished fondly.

"Shall we?" Brandon rose then discreetly helped Benjamin to his feet.

"Ladies," Benjamin said with a sweeping gesture of his hand, "After you."

Alex followed Allison and Ann Louise out of the room, and behind her, arm and arm strolled Brandon and Benjamin, speaking in jovial hushed voices. As they walked toward the formal dining room, Alex wondered at the fortitude of this family and so many others who had witnessed and experienced similar atrocities, not sure what to make of it. Then, she remembered something.

She'd once asked her grandfather about his experiences in Texas during Jim Crow and how he'd been able to survive, especially as a newspaper man, running the only black newspaper in the county. He'd paused, considered the question carefully then responded, his deep voice rolling over her like a gentle wave of comfort, as he counted off with his fingers, "God. Family. Faith. Patience. Love." He'd then balled his hand into a fist. "Combined, they're a powerful force against even the most hateful of folks."

Alex smiled to herself. She hadn't quite understood what he'd meant then, but now in the midst of a family who embodied these five ideals, she finally did. It also solidified another concept for her—karma. If not for brave men like Dr. George and her grandfather, proud black men willing to stand strong in the face of the injustices suffered by Tommy Lee and the countless others like him, there wouldn't be a Brandon George or Allison Sinclair-George willing to fight for justice and, thank God, win.

A Time Remembered

Leslie Perry

The elderly Black man with dark, rough skin and short Afro styled gray hair proudly strolls out of his small apartment and up the street to the school where he will help make history. He is from another generation that seems so long ago. When he was a boy, show fare was twelve cents and bus fare only a nickel. He was an eyewitness to air raids and sugar rations during the big war. His family was too poor to buy war bonds, but he remembers the time when fundraising would take place in movie theaters and he would put his pennies in the collection plate when it passed by him.

He also remembers that Black folks lived on one side of town and whites on the other. And the side where the whites lived was so much better than where the Blacks lived. And he remembers when television came on the scene and how mesmerized he and his family were with this new entertainment regardless of the fact that all the faces on the screen were white.

Some of his fondest memories were of Joe Louis, the Brown Bomber, battling it out in the boxing ring for race and country. He reflects on his family glued to the radio flinching at every blow that Joe took and the rejoicing when he came out the victor. Everyone in the house and the neighborhood celebrated. He thinks about Jackie Robinson breaking into the major leagues and how proud the entire Black race was because of one man's accomplishments. He thinks about the time the first Blackface appeared on television. Was it the "Beulah Show?" He's pretty sure it was.

He stops at the corner for a red light and watches as a car full of teenagers race by him. He thinks back to his teenage days. The terrible picture in *Jet* magazine of Emmett Till lying in the casket after being brutally murdered by some sadistic racist in the South appears in his mind. It brings back memories of the Civil Rights Movement. He didn't really get involved, but his heart and mind were with those who did. He flashes back on the Lincoln Monument and thousands of black and white faces standing on the Mall waiting for the one prophet of the time to speak. Even as a young man he was glued to his television that historic day in August 1963 when Dr. Martin Luther King Jr. told the world of his dream.

The light turns green and he continues across the street with a big smile. A major part of Dr. King's dream was about to happen today and he would be an active participant. But then the smile dissipates as he recalls the tragic event only a few weeks after Dr. King's speech. The entire Black world and a great many whites cried and mourned the loss of four beautiful Black girls and two brave Black boys who were tragically killed again by a bunch of minimalistic racists when the Sixteenth Street Baptist Church in Birmingham, Alabama, was bombed. On that tragic Sunday, he almost lost faith in mankind. But his better senses calmed him down and made him realize that evil is always going to make one last desperate attempt to destroy change for the better. Through Dr. King's work and the work of millions of other Americans, and especially the young brave Black children throughout the South, segregation was tumbling down just like the walls of Jericho.

He sees the school only a block away, and he is only a block away from helping achieve the dream. As he passes by an old white house where he lived back in 1957, he thinks of Little Rock, Ark. He recalls that day in September when nine brave Black boys and girls boldly crossed over the wedge of segregation and walked into Central High School, defying the mob and the racist Governor. All these events that now race through his mind like a thoroughbred horse racing to the finish line at the Kentucky Derby were necessary in order to make this day a reality.

He cried when he heard the news that Dr. King had been assassinated. He also felt hurt when two months later Bobby Kennedy met the same fate. He thought at that time, "What is happening in this country? Have our people all gone insane?"

He didn't' agree with the Vietnam War, but didn't protest, he didn't march, and didn't demonstrate. In a way, he wished he had. He knew some boys his age that didn't come back.

It took time before he adjusted to the natural hairstyle, dashiki, and the Black power slogans. It also took him some time before he stopped using the word Negro and started using Black. It was James Brown's song, "Say it Loud, I'm Black and I'm Proud" that changed him. He remembers very clearly how uncomfortable some of his white friends were with the Black and proud feeling among his people. When the whites became uncomfortable, he became comfortable. He even got his hair cut into a natural. He also had a girlfriend at the time that wore her hair in a natural. She was beautiful, proud, and smart. You had better not call her out of her name as happens today with young men and women. They even sing insulting songs to our sisters, something that never would have happened in the past.

He saunters onto the school grounds and heads toward the open double doors leading into the building. As he enters the building he thinks about the time when Jesse Jackson ran for president. He voted for him in the primaries in 1984 and again in "88." Even gave contributions to his campaign in both races. He also went to hear Jackson speak when he was in town. Jackson made him think about Dr. King when he spoke. But he also thinks about Shirley Chisholm who made a run for the presidency almost twenty years before Jackson. Very few give her credit for being bold, Black, and beautiful, taking such a step when her opposition was so strong.

He enters the auditorium and stands in line. It is a long line and it will take a while before they get to him. He doesn't care because this line stretches back over three hundred years and the wait is now about over.

These are his thoughts as he waits to get a ballot, and these are his thoughts as he enters the voting booth and pulls the lever associated with the name Barack Obama for President.

PASSING THE TORCH
Margaret Richardson and Lenton Collins

On the day of the funeral, Maximillan Massai Warner III stood at the foot of the hill and watched the sun come up over the pond below him. He felt the cool breeze tickle across his face. Massai, as family and friends called him, was dressed in a black three-piece suit, vest and all, with patent leather Stacy Adams. Grandpa had always told him that it was important to always look your best, especially at church.

"Starting the day," Grandpa said in his deep voice, "and dressing your best, even when the clothes are safety pinned together, always seems to put a little extra spring in your step."

Especially, on this particular day, Massai made sure that he looked his best. And he did look handsome, with his high cheekbones and dimples in both cheeks. His suit was perfectly cut for his broad shoulders and long legs. His wildly swirled purple and black tie was a perfect fit. Grandpa had given him the watch snuggly fitting on his wrist seven years ago and he wore it every day. Grandpa was not one for a lot of jewelry, just his watch and wedding band. All dressed and ready to go, Massai looked like his father and Grandpa before him, proud, dignified and strong.

He slowly strolled down the hill and sat at the bank of the pond. He picked up a rock, skipped it across the water and smiled, thinking back to the day that Grandpa taught him the art of skipping rocks across the pond. Grandpa was a pro, slinging the rock so that it would literally walk on its way to the bottom. With no more than a flick of the wrist and twist of his hand, he made aquatic art and Massai could never quite emulate that same fluid movement.

Coming to this spot always made him feel at home. Sitting there, he couldn't keep the tears from freely flowing down his face. He was at his favorite place in the world, alone and missing the one person who loved the pond more than he did. Massai had spent many a day at that very place with Grandpa fishing and just chewing the fat.

Grandpa always had a story to tell, always long and always about learning a lesson. Massai listened and paid close attention; indeed, he had no other choice. The one time he fell asleep and started snoring, Grandpa slapped him upside his head with his big hands that covered one entire side of his face. The slap was so loud Massai swore he heard an echo. He smiled and touched the spot where he had been slapped and awakened from his slumber.

"Black people always caught short and forever complaining about something, but always sleeping when they should be listening," Grandpa said after waking him up. "Never let anyone catch you sleeping. Always pay attention because you never know when something might happen that can be used to your advantage."

After that, Massai never fell asleep around him again.

One day while they were fishing, Grandpa told Massai about a similar trip he made down to the pond with Massai's daddy, Max, when he was only fourteen years old. Max hated fishing and complained every time Grandpa started toward the pond. He grumbled and muttered under his breath that, "Dad must not have anything else to do."

Grandpa just smiled and grabbed his rod and reel and a bag of sandwiches.

"Get the bait, the cooler, and tackle box," Grandpa said. They made it to the pond just as the sun was going down.

After setting up camp, Grandpa baited the hook with an earthworm and threw out his reel. Max didn't want to use live bait because he hated the way the earthworm wiggled in his hands. He threw his line out into the water without bait.

"Get that line in and bait your hook," Grandpa scowled when he saw what Max had done.

Max knew better than to cross Grandpa when he spoke. He obeyed and pulled his line back, baited his hook, and recast it, all the time grumbling under his breath. He was miserable and reasoned that if he looked miserable, surely his father would see it and release him from the hell he suffered out there.

But his father knew exactly what he was doing and couldn't have cared less. They were going to spend some time together if it killed them and he wasn't about to let Max spoil his fun. Grandpa started whistling "April in Paris." He nodded his head and moved his feet in time with the song, reaching the climax and starting it all over again. He finished the second time with a smile on his face. Grandpa looked at Max and said.

"That was Count Basie, one of the greats." He paused, glanced at his son and changed the subject. "School's almost out. What you planning on doing for the summer?" He worried about Max because his attitude was changing with age. He was always sullen, talked back, and generally got on everyone's nerves, even his mother.

"I'm hoping that I'll get that fellowship for the summer to study piano." Max was a gifted pianist and spent every minute of his spare time practicing. In fact, he'd rather be practicing right then instead of trying to catch fish. A frown crossed his face as he watched his father pull in his third fish.

Grandpa caught that frown. "You got to give the fish something they can catch on to," he instructed his son. "They like live bait. They snatch it up like lightning."

Max reasoned that fish couldn't move that fast, but he didn't care. He was, however, smart enough not to debate his father on the merits of using live bait.

Grandpa continued, "Once you cast the line, you'll have to wait a bit before the fish feels frisky enough to play. Take your time and wait it out. You have all the time in the world."

Max didn't care about all that and tried not to think about catching a fish, even though he'd never actually caught one before.

Suddenly, the line bucked a bit, bringing Max out of his musing. The line kept bucking and the reel almost slipped from his hand.

Grandpa looked over at him, and with his line still out in the water, calmly walked Max through reeling in the fish.

"Reel it in. Pull back a little," he said. "But not too much. Reel it in. Don't let go. Don't let go. Ride with it, Max." He was now shouting. He helped his son with the reel and smiled as Max began laughing at his success.

After getting the fish out of the water, Max watched as it bucked back and forth, trying to free itself from the hook. In spite of himself, Max was proud because he gave the fish the fight of its life and won.

Grandpa looked on with pride as Max celebrated his victory.

"Congratulations, Warrior, you have won a good fight," he said.

Max smiled at Grandpa and he smiled back at Max and, for a time, the unhappiness Max felt earlier had faded away. He handed Grandpa the fish who then dropped it in the water cooler.

Grandpa sat down and rested for a minute, setting the fishing rod down next to him. "How you feel after all of that action you went through to catch your first fish?"

Max stuck his chest out. "I feel good, strong, and fearless," he answered. Even though he had only caught a fish, he felt like he was a conqueror. Max couldn't keep the smile off his face.

Grandpa studied his son's reaction.

"And you did it all on your own," he said.

"I had help."

"But you didn't give up."

Grandpa closed his eyes and started whistling "April in Paris" again. He stopped momentarily. "Can you play 'April in Paris?'" he asked his son knowing that he could.

"Yes," Max answered with pride.

"Can you play 'Flying Home?'"

"No, but Lionel Hampton never played it on the piano," Max said.

Grandpa smiled. "A good musician can find a way to play a song on an instrument he had like that crazy Hendrix guy. Didn't he play the national anthem on his guitar?" He paused to let his knowledge sink in with his son. "It sounded like a bunch of noise, but I could tell the parts that mattered most. Now can you play 'Flying Home' on the piano?"

"No, I can't," Max replied more emphatically.

"Maybe you ought to learn. Maybe you'll pick it up while you're at camp this summer. That is, if you feel like going."

Max couldn't believe his ears. He looked at his father but couldn't say anything. He wanted to go to camp but wasn't sure if Grandpa would let him.

Grandpa smiled and after a long silence asked, "You think you'll be able to learn to play that song?"

Max, with a grin across his face, shook his head yes.

"I know one thing," Grandpa said. "I must really want to hear you play 'Flying Home,' because you sure don't deserve to go to that camp, not after your behavior before we came out here."

Max looked on in wonder because he didn't think his father had heard his remarks about going fishing.

"Yes, I heard you this time, the last time, every time you utter something you shouldn't, I hear it. I don't say anything about it because I hope that you'll see and understand that your behavior hurts me and your mama when it shouldn't."

With his head bowed Max asked, "Why you letting me go if I don't deserve it?"

"Maybe you need a rest from us and we need a rest from you."

"Is that how you feel?"

"Not really, but me and your mama know something got to change with your attitude. Maybe going to summer camp will give you a chance to find yourself and stop sulking all the time." Grandpa stared intently into his son's face hoping that his words would register with him. "And besides that, I want to hear you play 'Flying Home' for me and your mama when you get back."

Unable to hold back his emotions, tears filled Max's eyes. "I promise you."

"And it better be good just like you better be good. Next time you show out, I'll take you to the Marine recruiter myself, I don't care if you are under age, you'll be in the Marines and then let's see you act up."

They both sat back and laughed, luxuriating in the peace between them.

Grandpa told Massai a million times about how he and Max bonded on that fishing trip. Massai thought about his father and how he often treated him that very same way. He could see pieces of Grandpa in his father as well as in himself. He knew that they were all spades of the same color and it amazed him that Grandpa could tell exactly what Massai was thinking, even before he could get it out. Massai's son, Max IV, acted just like those before him, both hardheaded and stubborn. But what tickled Massai was that he would be able to tease his father about stories Grandpa used to tell him about how Max grew up.

Sharing the pond was the best gift of all. It was a family treasure that stayed with them at Grandpa's insistence. One time when Dad talked about possibly selling or leasing the land out, Grandpa would assert his right of possession. It was Grandpa's land and he intended that it be passed down through generations. No one was to break this inheritance, and he worked doggedly to make sure that the land was well cared for and the pond always full of fish. Max and Massai came to love the pond as much as Grandpa wished and Massai hoped that his son would love it as well.

Massai glanced at his watch. He still had some time before he had to do what he most dreaded in life. A petal glowing on a lily caught his attention. Calla lilies—beautiful colors of fuchsia, sunshine, and magenta mixed with the greenery of the lush grass and sparkling turquoise of the pond. Massai closed his eyes and listened to the birds singing with the breeze lifting hair on their throat. Right there at that moment, Massai felt as if he were in paradise. The day was shaping up to be a beautiful one, even though Massai dreaded what he would be doing. Having a funeral on a day like this one saddened him and took some of his joy away.

He continued thinking about the many times Grandpa talked with him at the pond. Grandpa always had stories to tell, some good, some bad, but always life changing in some way. The few stories Massai told always brought a laugh from Grandpa. He laughed because Massai's stories always bordered on the outrageous and strange like something from a science fiction movie. One time, Grandpa tried to verify one of Massai's stories with Max, who would just shake his head and apologize for his son's large imagination. Max thought of some of the humdingers he used to tell and wondered why Grandpa always laughed, even when he knew that many of them were made up.

Massai understood then that just like Grandpa could read his mind, he could also see right into his soul. Grandpa knew when Massai was telling the truth, pulling a fast one or riding the fence. And maybe he felt a little sorry for Massai and made up stories when just talking about life was always more interesting.

The funeral would take place in a couple of hours. The family was still getting up, eating breakfast, and dressing. The funeral director would pick up the family, and Massai hoped that the pastor wouldn't be late. He was habitually late for everything, funerals, weddings, and all other events at the church. He always had a reason, though, but no one cared enough to challenge the validity of his excuses. Maybe the pastor was putting his stories together like Massai used to do, but he couldn't imagine someone as old as him still watching the Saturday morning cartoons. In any case, Massai knew that he had time before he needed to be back at the house, so there was no need to rush.

He stood up and took a flower off the stem. He twirled it in his fingers and looked intently at the flower as if searching for an answer to one of life's mysteries. Massai brought it up to his nose to catch the familiar fragrance it held within its pedals. As he took it in, he thought back two years ago when his Grandma died. That was a bad time for the family. As much as Grandpa was the spiritual head of the family, Grandma was its backbone, and she held Grandpa's heart in the palm of her hand. She had been sick for a while but no one knew about it until just before she took to her bed in the final days.

Grandma was a big woman, six feet tall, over two hundred pounds with big feet and big hands. She had deep brown eyes, caramel skin, and a smile that lit up the room. Grandpa fell in love with her at first sight, but she couldn't stand the sight of him. Grandma could be intense. She was a serious person and more mature than her years. Her parents died early, leaving her to raise her younger sister and brother. She worked the farm by herself all day while still going to school. She struggled with her siblings for two years before her uncle popped up out of nowhere and took custody of her brother, who died a year later. No one was ever sure of the circumstances, only to say that John didn't want to be with Uncle Oliver in the first place.

Grandma was very close to her younger sister and had just sent her off to college when Grandpa came into her life. She was at a college dance and he asked her to dance. She said no, but Grandpa was the only one who could make Grandma smile. He was naturally good-humored, intelligent with a wonderful personality and eventually he grew on her. He would ask her to dance again at another school event, and this time she accepted. Grandpa couldn't dance a step but she let him lead and they eventually began to date. Grandma held him at bay long enough to see how serious he was about building a life with her. Once she was convinced that he was serious, the marriage took place and they spent the next fifty-two years dancing together.

The first sign that something was wrong with Grandma happened during a family reunion. She was preparing a huge pot of chicken and dumplings. She sat the pot on the stove and turned to put the pan of cornbread on the table. The other women in the kitchen thought that she simply lost her footing and fell against the stove. Maybe she was just tired. After all, she had also finished the potato salad, the broccoli and rice casserole, the cornbread stuffing, homemade rolls, pumpkin bread, two lemon meringue pies, a German chocolate cake, a red velvet cake, and a big bowl of banana pudding.

Grandpa said that she was doing too much and needed to rest. She wasn't hurt, but this had never happened before. One only had to know Grandma to understand that she moved deliberately and methodically, never wasting unnecessary steps.

Grandma did manage to get some rest but she never could get her footing right after her little accident. Anytime she was asked what was wrong she joked that old Arthur had finally caught up to her. The kids wanted to know who old Arthur was, but everyone over the age of thirty knew. Arthritis was an acquaintance that always seemed to drop in on people when they least needed to see him. And so, it was with Grandma that she let people believe old Arthur had found a home with her. But it was a lie, a merciful lie.

Grandpa knew something was wrong and took her to the doctor after she fell again. Kicking and scratching all the way, Grandma complained and cursed Grandpa the whole way back. Grandpa just looked at her and said,

"I love you more than life itself. I cannot and will not stand by and watch you fade away without knowing what's going on. So, you'll just have to complain. It's worth it to me to make sure you're okay."

She stopped complaining and turned away from him, but not before she saw the tears fall from his eyes.

Cancer. It's an ugly word with an ugly meaning. In those days of cancer treatment, the destination was always the same and it was a painful ride all the way. Grandma had it in her blood and it caused her to get weaker and weaker. She tried to keep pace, working as she always did, taking care of her family, and watching her grandchildren grow up. She took care of Grandpa and helped him take care of the pond. But her steps grew slower, her handshake grew weaker, her smile waned, and the light slowly faded from her eyes. She could no longer stay at the pond with Grandpa because the breeze would drift right through her.

Grandpa did what he could to comfort her, but he looked on with increasing despair. He was slowly losing his wife. The knowledge that she was fading away pained him more than he let on. He tried to keep her spirits up and keep her laughing. He told some of the weirdest jokes, always acting out the parts so that she could see the punch line. She did laugh, but not because the jokes were funny. The jokes were stale, but Grandpa worked so hard to entertain her that she laughed just to see him smile.

Grandma held on for two years. She was in a lot of pain and there was nothing that could be done. Everyone knew that her condition was serious but she never let on just how serious it was. She didn't want people feeling sorry for her or looking at her with pity. She'd decided that she had lived her life as she wanted to and had no regrets. She didn't like the pain she had to endure, but she was ready for whenever God called her home.

One night she set her hair, now completely gray and thinning. She put on a gown and set out a suit for Grandpa to wear. On top of the suit was a note, asking for his attendance to a private dance, to begin as soon as he was present. She gingerly walked to the living room and found one of her favorite pieces, "Moonlight Serenade." Then she changed her mind when she came across "It Had to be You." She sat down and waited for her groom to arrive.

Grandpa went to the bedroom and instead of finding Grandma, he found the suit on his bed with the note. He followed the instructions and went to the living room to see what would happen. When he got there, he found Grandma on the love seat waiting for him. He couldn't believe his eyes. She was a vision in her lavender gown with her silver hair coiffed beautifully. She had a bit of rouge on and held a calla lily in her hand. He smiled his biggest smile and couldn't hold back the tears that flowed.

When Grandma saw Grandpa standing in the doorway, she also smiled.

"Come and sit with me," she said in a low, weak voice.

He strolled over to the love seat and sat close to her.

"You look so handsome," she said.

"And you are as beautiful as that first day I saw you at the school dance."

She blushed. "Thank you. Would you dance with me?"

His voice choked, "It would be my pleasure." He stood up and reached for her hand. He pulled her up and walked her to the middle of the room.

He held her and they danced for the first time in years. They stayed close and reminisced about their life. They joked, laughed, and danced, enjoying their time together.

Finally, they walked to the pond and sat under the moonlight. When it grew too cold, Grandpa wrapped his suit jacket around her and they snuggled like they used to do. After a time, they walked back to the house and went to bed. Laying there, holding her close and still feeling good from the night's activities, Grandpa started whistling "April in Paris."

Grandpa still held her the next morning. He kissed her cheek and tried to wake her but she didn't move. She'd slipped away during the early morning without a shake or shudder. She was at peace, her face showing no pain or stress, quiet in the arms of the one she loved most. Grandpa embraced her with all his energy and love, then started to cry. He stayed there with her alone for a very long time, but finally realized their time on this side of the mountain was over.

He alerted Max, and Grandma was taken away. But Grandpa remained in their bedroom and held on to her pillow still fresh with the scent of her perfume. It was clear from all who saw him from that moment on he had just lost his best friend. Friends and family began to gather around him and everyone paid their condolences as best they could. The days before her funeral were a blur, but everyone agreed that Grandpa and Grandma had a love story that few will ever know. Grandpa was silent throughout, never uttering more than a couple of words for hours.

Grandma's sister, Olivia, sat with him. Olivia and Massai were the only two Grandpa wanted near him. Max and his brothers, Mitchell and Matthew, took care of the arrangements while his sisters, Marguerite and Marie Rose, took care of the guests.

Maureen May Oliver Warner was put away beautifully and laid to rest next to her parents and her brother John.

After everyone left the house, Grandpa walked to the pond. He had been there for over three hours by the time Massai finally caught up with him. Like everyone else, Massai was worried about Grandpa.

"How you holding up?" he asked.

Grandpa remained silent for a long moment. In fact, he was too quiet for too long.

"Grandpa, you all right?"

Grandpa smiled and looked at his grandson. "Yeah, I'm okay."

Massai knew better. There was no way he felt all right, not after just burying the most important person in the world to him.

Grandpa must have been reading Massai's thoughts. "Yes, your grandmother has passed on. She is no longer of this world and I miss her more than you will ever know. But I am humbled by what we shared, this life one earth and everything that came with it, both the good and the bad."

Grandpa picked up a stone and tossed it across the top of the water as only he could do.

"She was my earth, wind, and fire. She was all of the elements I needed to survive and my life will never be the same without her." A tear rolled down his cheek, but still he smiled. He wanted to remember his dance of fifty-two years with the love of his life rather than to focus on the slow pain his beloved endured to the end.

Grandma's passing was a while ago, seven years and six months exactly. Massai couldn't know how much Grandpa hurt every day since then. To begin the next day after your beloved has departed is rough, especially if you were together for what seemed like an eternity. Massai yearned to help Grandpa, but hoped that one day he would know of the special love that his grandparents obviously shared together. He was always amazed at how Grandpa could see a blessing in any circumstance or misery. He also wondered how Grandpa lived out his last days missing Grandma as much as he did. He would always say, "You live each day as it comes, one minute at a time. It makes no sense to try and predict what will happen or if something might happen. All you can do is to live each moment as if it were your last. You do that and you won't have so much to worry about." It sounded like good advice so Massai followed it, making it his own code of survival.

Massai checked his watch again. It was time to join the family inside. He walked from the pond back to the house where his wife, Malia, waited for him.

"You okay?" she asked as she took his hand and held it tightly.

"Yes."

"What were you doing down at the pond all this time?"

"I was with Grandpa."

They walked hand in hand over to Max and Max IV. Malia took her son's hand and walked away while Massai hugged his father. Max was now elevated as the patriarch of the family and his shoulders were heavy with bereavement for the loss. He was without his mother or father and felt like an orphan, even at his age. He and his son headed out of the house and to the limousines waiting to take the family to the church.

On the way to the church, they all sat still, caught in the maze of their own emotions. The only time they laughed was when Max IV grabbed himself and said,

"Mommy, I got to potty."

"Hold on for just a few more minutes and we'll be at the church," Malia whispered.

He was able to hold on until they reached the church, and Malia rushed him to the restroom while the rest of the family assembled in the foyer. Once the family was all gathered, they walked into the sanctuary, strolled by the open casket and paid their respects to Maxmillan Massai Warner Senior, the man they knew as Dad and Grandpa. The family took their seats and waited for Pastor Washington to get the service started.

Massai wished they'd gotten someone other than Pastor Washington to officiate over Grandpa's home going service. The good pastor was all right enough, Massai supposed. But he drank like a fish and felt the need to get up in your face to say something. You always needed to wipe off after a conversation with him and also ask if he wanted a Tic Tac. Besides that, Pastor Washington tended to be nosy, and if you weren't paying close attention, you'd think he nodded off during his sermons. Massai remembered one time when Pastor Washington went into a rant about something he accused Max of doing. Max explained that the circumstance was a misunderstanding, but Pastor Washington wouldn't let it go. Everyone got the message, but not Pastor Washington. After losing his patience over Washington asking the same question, Max snapped, got right in the minister's face, and shouted.

"Are you stupid or just ignorant?"

Pastor Washington didn't know how to respond, but it shut him up. Needless to say, he never messed with Max again. Massai laughed at the memory and looked at Max, winking his eye at him as they saw Pastor Washington coming in.

The service began with the pastor reading "Psalms 23" and then offering a ten-minute prayer. Grandpa would have said that it was too long—that God didn't need to hear all of that if the prayer was genuine. Mitchell and Marie Rose did a duet, "In the Upper Room." Grandpa loved that song and asked his children to do it right.

Next, Matthew gave his remembrance of Grandpa. He told stories about how Grandpa grew up as an only child, how he met his wife, and was the kind of father that his children admired and looked up to.

"As a father, Dad put the fear of God into us early because we were some bad children," Matthew said. "He wanted to make sure that we remembered that anytime God is put into the equation, the outcome will always be what you need it to be." Matthew finished up as Marguerite came up.

Before Marguerite reached the pulpit, Pastor Washington was on his feet offering another prayer and started to sing, but Marguerite politely asked him to sit down. She thanked Pastor Washington for his heartfelt friendship during her family's time of loss. She reminisced that what Grandpa always talked about was how involved Pastor Washington was in the lives of his members and how much the good pastor meant to the community. Massai could hear people snickering and he started to laugh as well because they were well aware how Grandpa felt about the good pastor.

Marguerite got so carried away that she had to catch herself from calling Pastor Washington Reverend Such and Such. Grandpa had given him that nickname after the good pastor came over to the house, ate up most of the food, and interfered in Grandpa's business once too often. Marguerite wrapped up her remarks and sat down, smiling all the while.

Massai finally got up to do the eulogy. He didn't know what he could say that might do the man he called his best friend justice.

"We come together today to bury our beloved father, grandfather, and friend, Maxmillan Massai Warner Senior. He was a God-fearing man who took care of his family, took care of his community, and tried to be the best he could be." Massai didn't know how to say the rest. He looked at his father who sent him looks of encouragement. "Grandpa was the man we all looked up to. He was our role model, our leader, our teacher, and our friend. He taught us that to be a good Black man, you didn't have to wear it on your sleeve. To be a good Black man, you didn't have to beat up anyone or yourself to prove that you were a man. You didn't have to prove anything except to yourself. You owe it to yourself to be the best that you can be. Take care of your responsibilities, always stay around to finish the job you started, and accept no less." Massai took in a deep breath to keep from choking up. "He taught us to always give as much as you receive and you never let anyone say that you are worthless. My grandfather gave me the self-worth of understanding that I am a warrior, not a thug, not an animal, but a human being." This time Massai paused to look directly at his father and force a smile. "Through my father, my grandfather let me know that I am priceless and valuable as a human being, as a Black man, and as one of God's children. If I am half the man my grandfather was, I'll consider it a victory for which he deserves the credit."

Massai grabbed the sides of the pulpit to help keep him up. His legs wobbled because with every word he spoke he realized just how important Grandpa had been to him and the overwhelming magnitude of their loss. He also knew that all over the country, services were being conducted just like this one, and he could only pray that the person who was being eulogized meant just as much to his or her family as Grandpa meant to the Warner family. He continued:

"Our lives were enriched through Grandpa's presence. We were all made richer because we saw the example he set with his children, his grandchildren, and all the people he loved. He wasn't afraid of hard work. He wasn't afraid of saying no when you hoped he'd say yes. And he wasn't afraid of saying yes when he should have said no. He protected us, taught us, and wasn't afraid to discipline us when we needed it. He pushed us, cheered for us, and wasn't afraid to cry with us when we cried. I said earlier that we have come together to bury our loved one, but I was wrong. We have come together to celebrate a life that touched us all, a life as precious as the earth, wind, and fire it took to help him survive. All our lives have been made better for the dues he paid and the road he paved for us to travel along. I know that he loved us as much as we loved him.

"Lastly, I say to my grandpa, my best friend, Maximillan Massai Warner Senior, well done my beloved warrior. God knows that you have fought the good fight, won your victory, and deserve your reward. We love you."

Massai walked from the pulpit down to where Max sat and hugged him. Massai never noticed until just then how much his father resembled Grandpa in looks, spirit, and temperament, although Max was a lot quieter than Grandpa was.

Max got up and strolled up to his father's casket, stopped, and placed his hand on the side. He then continued over to the piano. Max took a deep breath and placed his hands on the keys. He always did that when he was about to begin. He closed his eyes and touched the keys to one of his father's favorites, "Mary Don't You Weep," bringing the congregation to their feet. Max truly had a precious instrument in his voice although the piano was slightly out of key. It didn't matter because Max knew what he was doing. He played the piano like a virtuoso. No one was even aware that the piano was off key. He opened his eyes as he finished the song, but couldn't get up.

Max sat there, thinking he needed to do something else. He looked back at the casket and said under his breath, "Dad, this is for you." He played "Flying Home" just as his father had once asked him to do. He'd never gotten the opportunity to play it once he returned from the summer camp. He and Grandpa had forgotten about the request, at least he had. Maybe Grandpa had been waiting for him to live up to his promise. He never would have asked him because he shouldn't have to. Max decided that even if he were doing it a little late, his father would get his request filled. The tears continued to flow as he worked his way through the song. He cried because he knew somewhere his father was smiling. He was right, Max could play "Flying Home" on the piano, just like Grandpa thought he could all of those years before.

Max finished and bowed his head still sitting at the piano. His brothers, sisters, and his son Massai hurried up to the piano and hugged him. They all walked back to the pew together. Pastor Washington tried to say another prayer, but Mitchell stopped him. The service came to an end and they marched out to the limousines preparing for the ride to the cemetery. Pastor offered to ride in the lead car with Max and his family, but they pushed him up to ride with the funeral director in the hearse.

When they arrived at the cemetery, Mitchell, Max, Matthew, Massai, Massai's brother Michael, and cousin Deacon carried the casket to its final resting place. After placing the casket on the hoist for lowering into the ground, the boys took their place alongside Marguerite and Marie Rose and waited for Pastor Washington to catch up. The pastor said another prayer, but kept it short this time after Mitchell warned that he would not get paid for officiating the service if he didn't. The family together recited the Lord's Prayer quietly, and the pallbearers took turns throwing their roses into the grave.

Max sauntered over to his mother's grave. He whispered:

"Okay, Mom, you're together again. Dad's ready but you'll have to lead. Enjoy your dance." Max turned and walked back to the limousine where the family waited for him.

The procession returned to the main house. Max IV was given free reign to play since he'd been so good all day. He somehow managed to charm great Aunt Olivia and they became friends. Some church members came over and helped take care of the guests. There was enough food given to the family for three funerals and everyone filled up fast except Pastor Washington who seemed to have a bottomless pit for a stomach. In the end, the leftovers were given to Pastor Washington.

Massai slipped out and sauntered down to the pond. It was the first place Grandpa and his father took him and the only place in the world he felt secure. He sat down at the bank and took off his shoes and socks, letting his toes play at the edge of the water. He loosened his tie and rolled up his sleeves to get even more comfortable.

"Grandpa, I know you hear me," he whispered. "Did you hear Dad play? He was amazing. Everyone was awesome except Pastor Washington. Aunt Marguerite almost called him Reverend Such and Such when she was speaking." Massai started laughing hard. "Washington is a piece of work," he continued. "I'm glad I don't have to deal with him. We gave him the rest of the leftovers. I hope he enjoys them." Massai was now rambling, but he had to do this because he didn't want to let go.

He remained quiet for a minute, then got up and reached for a calla lily. Taking one of the stems, he played with it in his fingers. He began again.

"You would have been proud of us today. We were a family. We leaned on each other just like you knew we would. We weren't afraid to cry." Massai looked around like he was waiting for Grandpa to walk up. He stared at the flower and said, "I know you told us that we're supposed to live each day as it comes, one minute at a time. I know that I can do the best I can and be the man I was raised to be. I want to make you proud of me. I'm going to be a good father to my son. I promise I won't be like other Black men, donating sperm to whatever girl they fancy for the moment."

Again, he paused to gather his thoughts. What he said was so important and he had to say it right. "I'm going to do so much for him and spend so much time with him that he'll get tired of looking at me. But however tired Max IV gets, he'll never be able to say that his father didn't love him or want him around."

Massai stood up as it all suddenly came together for him. He knew what he had to do and it amazed him that it took so long to see what was obvious. He laughed, shook his head, and said,

"Okay, Grandpa, I gotcha. I'll be right back." He went back to the house and got Max IV.

Massai brought Max IV back to the pond he'd fallen in love with long ago. He let his son run around and after Max IV sat down, Massai joined him. He took off his son's shoes and socks and let him splash in the water. Massai told Max IV that he was very young also when his father first took him to the pond. And his father was brought there by his father, renewing the cycle of a father sharing with his son a rich heritage and culture that was passed down from generation to generation.

Massai looked at his son, smiled, and hugged him. He released Max IV, promising to be the role model his son needed, just like his father and grandfather had been for him.

One Boy's Quest for Knowledge
D. L. Grant

The woman at the massive oak desk looked up unsmiling when the little boy walked into the building. Usually, it was her job to smile, answer questions, and help people find books. Standing outside the building, the boy observed her manner through the glass pane in the door as she interacted with two young girls who did not look like him. She smiled while dealing with the two girls.

She was still smiling when he first walked into the building, but when she looked into his brown eyes and at his dark skin her smile dissipated. It was replaced with a smirk and it caused the boy's stomach to tighten and his blood to rush to the top of his head causing him to feel dizzy. He had walked a long way to reach this place. He wanted to reach out and hold on to one of the two massive columns that led through the foyer and into the building. He started to extend his hand but thought better of it. Somehow that single act seemed as though it would be worse, more intrusive than stepping all the way inside the building.

You don't have to touch. Not right now. One day you will.

Stepping inside the building, the place smelled different than any place he had ever visited. He could not describe it but it was not unpleasant. Then it hit him. It was the smell of books. His excitement nearly overtook him. He made a tentative step in the direction of the reading room off to the left but decided against it. He took one step back. Better not look too familiar. He knew he wasn't supposed to be there. The woman who stopped smiling knew it, too. More than a hundred years of history, culture, and tradition screamed that he was not welcome inside. Then he remembered himself. He swallowed hard but did not turn and head for the door. His heart couldn't possibly beat any faster than it already was, but he had gone too far, sacrificed too much. The minute he set foot in the building he had been marked. He was already the little darkie that came into the library. Hatred would not lessen. The threshold had been sullied, compromised. Maybe they would burn the place down, start all over again. He felt other eyes on him and their stares were as cold and steely as the woman at the desk.

"I…" he stammered. "I…"

"May I help you?" Her voice was insistent. Her manner was meant to send him running.

He had endured the hateful eye from whites his entire young life. He knew it well. It shocked and it stunned, but it did not kill. It was not the look that did the killing. The look was the warning. It was a cautionary measure.

"Boy, do you want something? You can't have any water. And you know you can't use the bathroom."

Still, he said nothing. People stared up from their newspapers and books. Eyes peered from around the book stacks. His heart continued racing, and he was certain he could not have spoken a complete sentence if a script had been placed in his hands.

"No ma'am," he managed to stammer.

He stood his ground and looked around at the people whispering none too quietly. He could pick up snatches of conversation. Familiar words such as uppity, nigger, darkie pelted his back. Insults were of no consequences.

The boy stared up at the ceiling. It was high and vaulted. He drank in the sheer magnificence of the craftsmanship that was evident in the dark wood that framed the tall windows that seemed to go on forever. Painstaking artistry was everywhere, in the molding and carvings that adorned every wall within view, even in the portraits of old bearded men that hung here and there and sweeping landscapes that captured scenes of the state's past. It was the grandest place he had ever seen. It was like something he saw in the movies whenever he had a nickel to see one. And the books! Books were everywhere. The place was just as magnificent as he had imagined it must be and he had passed by it many times. He began to imagine the words and the images that must be contained in those books that were close enough for him to touch.

Finally, he glared back at her, no longer oblivious to the gentle echoes of hard shoes on the tiled floor. Their eyes met and seemed to communicate. Words unspoken passed between them. He was certain she knew what he was thinking. Like Adam in the Garden, his eyes became opened. Now he knew things. Unlike Adam he was not embarrassed. There was no apology in his eyes. He was not sorry for being there. Instead, he understood fully, as she did that an apology was owed to him because she had loved the books all along. She had to love them in order to come into a magnificent place like this day in and day out. But to not share them—and this building—with all the people was a sin of the most unconscionable kind!

The slightest hint of crimson tinged her hard face. Her back stiffened, she sniffed, pushed her glasses back up on her nose, and looked away. He had made his point and she knew it. A victory! He had scored one for every colored face she had turned away from the building. Still, she rallied. All she had was her hatred, and how would that serve her at judgment? Now, she meant to put him back in his place.

"I don't know why you're here. Are you lost? She asked defiantly. "There's nothing here for you." She realized the foolishness of her words. *Nothing here for you.*

The young boy regarded her again whispering to himself, "*Why does anyone come into a library?*"

She folded her arms and looked away impatient with his stubbornness.

He turned and walked out of the building. Head bent down, the boy headed home. He lifted his head to look over his shoulder now and again, wondering if anyone was following him.

That evening he sat down to a meal of beans, cornbread, and leftover collards. He was silent at the dinner table and the rest of the evening. His days were the stuff of the secret life of boys. There was, after all, the life of children that parents know and the life that they don't. Beyond the watchful gaze of parental eyes were old abandoned buildings that cried out to be explored, creeks to play in, and railroads to be followed in bare feet. This, too, he would keep to himself.

The next morning, he did not return to the library. He awoke, marveling to himself that the house had not burnt down while his family slept inside. Sunlight crept gently across the floor of the room he shared with his older brother. He was alive and had not received a beating from his father for…well, what could he be punished for? For quietly insisting that people give him something he knew he had a right to? Intellectually, he could not quite frame the thing that so occupied him. But what was as clear to him as his own name was the fact that no one should have access to something he could not have. Not if he could help it.

The following two days he did return to the library, stood in that same spot and received the identical stern stares from the lady as if warning him to do not dare enter. With each day his anger became more intense, his determination more dogged. Finally, on the fourth day he returned and received those same disapproving stares and heard the same whispers. It was this way the next day and the next. The woman, he figured, was the librarian in charge. She was the one who still asked in an impatient voice if she could help him. He never ventured very far away from the entrance. He would arrive, stay a few moments, then leave, careful to make sure no one was following him as he made his way home. Each night on those occasions he frequented the library, he sat nervously back at home eating dinner and wondering if anyone might ask about his clandestine visits to the library. When asked how he spent his day, he delivered his stock response, "Nothing much."

That summer of 1963, he didn't bother to read newspapers and was unaware of the demonstrations at segregated facilities upstate that resulted in numerous beatings and, in a couple of instances, deaths of colored folks who were demanding the same rights he sought at the library. Still, at some level, he perceived there could be danger in what he was determined to do. But he had come too far to give up what he had started. He was so close. So close. He was certain that he could change people's minds. He would help them to see that colored people were as good as other people. A boy reasons this way, believes he can change minds and erase boundaries long established, however unfair, by merely being good. For all his pluck, he still saw things the way a boy did. He did not understand that what was at stake was a way of life that now seemed threatened. *You give 'em the right to access, what would they ask for next?* He was unaware that the simple act of taking a seat in the all-white library was another blow to years of tradition.

He had returned to that library every day for a week and now on a scalding hot Friday, the first day of August, he decided it was going to be a day of action. Actually, the deal had been sealed the night before when he'd laid down his head to go to sleep. When he awoke that morning, he found that he was too excited to eat so he bypassed the plate of breakfast food prepared for him and now was sitting on top of the kitchen stove. He dawdled around the house, waiting for his older brother to leave, also headed to points unknown. Then he made his own move.

The young boy with frayed nerves was out of the house and down the street, headed toward the place where he would make his demand known and would in doing so force justice to be tested. Destiny awaited him. Maybe it was cockiness. Maybe it was impatience. Maybe still it was the incredulity of the situation—denying colored people the right to use the library. Whatever it was, the time had come for the ultimate act of defiance, and it had to be today. He had tired of walking the long distance to the library, just to turn and walk away. The people should be used to him by now. They should know that he was not going to cause problems or make a mess. He could sit quietly and behave just like all of the others who used the library. Indeed, today was the day he would make the ultimate demand. He would have a seat in the white man's library, open a book, and read.

Small balls of sweat rolled down his face as he walked up the ten steps that led into the building. He was hot but it didn't matter. All that mattered waited on him inside the pillars of the building. The boy strolled with pride inside the building and instantly locked eyes with the woman at the desk. By now he was certain that she was the person in charge. Whereas once he thought he might have sensed a hint of resignation, he now saw a decided look of determination in her hard-blue eyes. Perhaps she had awakened with the same sense of purpose as he. It was strange the way it seemed she could read his mind and determine his motive. He swallowed hard. Yes, here I am again, he thought. His eyes fixed on hers, he stepped gingerly in the direction of the nearby reading room.

In an instant the woman came around her desk and blocked his path. Calmly, he started around her but she moved to block him again. He again attempted to make his way to the reading room. They just looked at each other.

"Don't you know anything?" Her voice was but a whisper and he was not certain if he had heard her correctly. She was almost pleading with him. "Leave now."

He was trying to figure out what to do next when he was given a hard shove from the back.

"You really don't know what kind of danger you are in, do you, boy?" A harsh, deep voice said suddenly, catching him off guard.

He had not heard the man approach. The nearness and forcefulness of his voice made the boy jump. He turned to confront a red-faced man with angry gray eyes.

"Otherwise you wouldn't be in here where you are not wanted. Where you don't belong," the man continued.

The boy was too afraid to move.

The man removed the belt from around his waist and held it close to the boy's countenance.

"You see this, boy? I could wrap this belt around your neck and drag your nigger behind out of this building and hang you from that tree over yonder. No one would care." The man bent close to the boy and spoke softly. "You know what they're doing to uppity Negras like you up in Shuler County? Do you want to hang from that tree?"

Still, the boy could not speak or move. But he was aware that some customers had begun to rise from their tables and were looking on. He could hear the scrapings of oak chairs as still others vacated their seats to see what was going on. Suddenly, no plot in any book was as compelling as what was taking place right before their eyes.

He had never seen this man in the library before. Though he was a stranger to the boy, there was no mystery about him. The sight of a little colored boy trying to break customs much older than he, customs that had been necessary to maintain the proper relationship between superior and inferior human beings, evidently repulsed the man, and the boy knew he meant to do harm to him.

For the first time the boy felt doubt and the doubt was mixed with fear. Had he overplayed his hand in his demand to have access to books? Before he could respond the man snatched him off his feet and lifted him a couple feet off the floor.

"Put me down," he cried. "Put me down!" Tears flooded his eyes as he struggled and kicked. He clutched at his neck and gasped for air.

The man was quite strong and his anger seemed to increase his strength. His knuckles dug into the boy's neck and limited his air supply.

"Put him down!" a woman's voice shouted. "Put him down!" The voice belonged to the woman who each day glared at him and who moments before had barred him from entering the reading room. "You will not harm a hair on his head. I will not allow you to disgrace this building with your brutish behavior. It's not right. This is not Shuler County."

The man stood his ground with the boy still hoisted in the air. He glared at the woman and she glared right back at him.

She wasn't about to back down, not when the dignity of the library was at stake. It represented something greater than the Southern tradition, the Southern ways. It represented civilization for hundreds of years and that had to be protected from this uncivilized intrusion.

The man finally dropped the boy back to the floor. The thrust forced him to his knees, but he quickly jumped back up.

The lady with the steely blue eyes and the hard stare, took his hand and walked him to an office, leaving the man huffing and puffing where he stood. The boy watched as the lady sat at a desk and inserted a small card into the roller of an old manual typewriter. Instead of typing anything on the card she looked down at the keys and then at him. She then took his hands in both of hers.

He stared into her eyes. She was older than he thought at first. Her blue eyes now seemed tired instead of hard.

"I want to tell you something," she said, words no longer harsh but soft and gentle. "I knew this day was coming. I just didn't know when or how or with what fanfare. I suppose I should thank you. North of town, over in Shuler County, people are being beaten and killed for attempting the same thing you were doing." For the first time since their confrontations, she smiled. "I love this library and no library should be a place where people fight and die. Seeing you here has made me know that the time has come. I am very sorry about what happened to you today." She squeezed his hands and then released them.

"You know all this time I haven't known your name, but now I must so that I can issue you a library card."

"Levi," the boy whispered still somewhat in shock.

"Your full name must be on your library card." She emphasized the "your."

"Levi Flood, ma'am."

She typed his name and said, "I don't know if I will have a job here tomorrow or if I will be asked to resign from my church. But I would like to give you something." She rolled the card out of the typewriter and handed him a library card that read La Fleur County Library with his name "Levi Flood" typed out below it. "Well, Levi Flood, let's go back inside and find those books that you like best."

THREE SHORT TALES AS TOLD BY
GRIOT LESLIE PERRY

The Door of No Return

People called her crazy. Her husband left her and took their three children with him. He took another woman as his wife and had two more children with her.

The woman the villagers called crazy lived just outside the village. Why they called her crazy was because of the things she said. She talked about being kidnapped and taken aboard a great ship. She talked about being rescued by a magical fish.

There was a time when she was a young teenage girl no different than any other girl in the village. But then one day she disappeared. Her father went hunting for her. Other men of the village joined him. They hunted several days, but could not find her. Her father never stopped hunting.

Months went by and her entire family, as well as the other members of the village, were heart broken. They had lost one of their own and they suffered as a family, just as when the occasion presented itself, they celebrated as a family. The occasion to celebrate came one day when the young girl suddenly appeared in the village. But she was different. Much more quiet and refused to talk with anyone. She only said that she was taken away. She did not say who took her or where she went.

A few years after she had returned, she was married. She gave birth to three children. Sometime after the birth of her last child, she began to tell a strange story that no one believed. And that is when her husband and other villagers began to call her crazy.

Because of her strange story she was forced to live alone in a small hut outside the village. Life has taken a toll on her and she looks much older than her actual age. It has been a long time since she first began to tell her strange story and now all three children are grown and have children of their own.

One day as Maleka, for that is her name, is cleaning her hut she looks up and there standing outside her doorway is a young girl.

"Hello," Maleka says.

The young girl says nothing

"I know who you are and I believe I know why you have come."

The young girl still does not speak.

"Come closer. I will not harm you, for you are my granddaughter."

How do you know who I am?"

"I have seen your mother and I have seen you with your mother. But I would know you anywhere. You carry my likeness with you."

"People say you are crazy," the little girl says.

"There are people who say that," Maleka agrees. "But I think it is best to learn on your own. Don't you think it is better to learn on your own…to really know things, and not believe what others have said?"

The young girl says nothing, but just stares directly into Maleka's eyes.

"Shall I tell you a story—the story some people don't believe—the story that some people think makes me crazy?"

Maleka detects some curiosity in the young girl's stare. She extends her hand and waves her into the hut.

"You can come a little closer if you wish."

The little girl stands her position and still does not speak.

Her stand-off nature does not deter Maleka. The time has finally come to tell her granddaughter what happened to her. Maybe she will also think Maleka is crazy, but the little girl has to know. Hopefully, it might make her a bit more cautious when wandering outside the safety and comfort of the village.

"It began a day like this." Maleka steps outside the doorway to be closer to her granddaughter. "I was just a few years older than you. I was getting wood for the fireplace. Do you sometimes get wood for your mother when she is cooking?" Maleka pauses hoping the little girl will open up to her. She does not and Maleka continues. "Well that is what I was doing.

"I wandered a little too far from my village and I saw people from another tribe coming at me. There were warnings among the elders of my village that some tribesmen from other villages would kidnap children. So as soon as I saw them, I started running. I could hear them behind me, and gaining on me. I could run fast as a young girl, but they still caught me. When they did, they bound me with rope and led me away—away from my village, away from my mother and father, away from all my friends." She pauses as tears well up in her eyes remembering that dreadful day.

"Several hours later I was taken to a place where there were other people who were also bound by ropes. They were bound around their wrists and necks and with ropes connecting one person to the next. I was bound together with this group of people.

"None of us said anything. The people who bound us spoke a language I had never heard before. But I knew what they were saying by their shouts and gestures was not good for me."

Her granddaughter moves a step closer to Maleka and allows her to place a hand on her shoulder. It is the first time she has ever touched this little girl who means so much to her. She feels a chill.

"The first night we slept on the ground in the night air. We were not given any food or any water. Early in the morning we were led away. I do not remember how long we walked or how far, but it seemed that we walked forever.

"Finally, we came to a dungeon. Men with a strange skin color—a color I had never seen before, met us. They looked us over very carefully. Then we were taken into the dark, damp, and cold dungeon. Once we were inside the ropes were taken off and we were all chained together." Maleka stretches out both arms and cuffs her hands simulating the manner in which they were chained. It is all very difficult for her to do, but it has to be done so that her granddaughter will understand. All the children of the village need to hear her story, but they think she is crazy.

"Do you know what chains are?" she continues. "They serve the same purpose as ropes. Only you can't cut them and you can't break them."

Maleka feels the young girl warming up to her so she leads her into the hut. She sits on a stool inside. Telling this story and recalling all the horror tires her out. The little girl sits on the floor near her.

"I cried many tears in that place. Oh, how I cried. We stayed there for many days. The food we ate was not like the fresh food that comes from the earth or the fruits that come from the trees or the fish from the rivers. The food we ate had a strange smell and a strange taste and that made it hard to swallow." Maleka simulates swallowing to demonstrate.

"At night I could hear the lapping sounds of water hitting the walls of the dungeon. Sometimes I smelled water—a great body of water. And then one day a door opened that had never been opened before. And each of us were led out of that door."

Maleka smiles. She really loves this child, her granddaughter.

"Where did the door go to?"

"To a world of no return," Maleka says. "Actually, we boarded a boat. A very large boat. But we had to go down into the belly of the boat. And we were forced to lie down like slabs of wood, one person lying down next to the other with barely enough room to twist or turn around and no room to lift up our heads because the ceiling was only inches from our faces. Each of us was chained to the person next to us."

"Did you have to sleep that way?" the young girl questions.

Maleka's smile broadens. Her granddaughter is talking with her asking questions, unlike the adults in the village who call her crazy. "Would you mind if I call you granddaughter?"

The young girl nods her head. "You can call me granddaughter."

"To answer your question, Granddaughter, that's how we had to stay at all times, lying side by side, day after miserable day. For a short time each day, we would be unchained and marched up to the top of the boat. Drums would be beaten and we would be forced to jump around as if we were dancing to the drums. Then we would be marched down again to the belly of the boat, to the foul smell and the darkness, always the darkness." She pauses to catch her breath. A feeling comes over her similar to the feelings she had in the darkness.

"One night a person lying not far from me stopped breathing. He lay there all night and in the morning one of the men on the boat unchained him and dragged his body away. He was buried in the waters." Maleka's body trembles all over. Her voice cracks. "One night, or day, I don't remember, I was unchained and taken to a room where the man in charge of the boat stayed. He did something to me that hurt very badly. The next day or night I was taken to this room again. And the next night and many nights after that."

"What did he do to you?"

"Very terrible things that children shouldn't know about," Maleka answers abruptly. She doesn't mean to be short with her granddaughter, especially since the child is opening up to her, but what happened in that room night after night shouldn't be told to a child.

She changes the subject. "During my days on that boat I had seen some poor souls jump into the water. They were not jumping to swim to safety. We were too far from land to do that. They were jumping for another reason."

"To die?"

"Yes, to die," Maleka answers in a subdued tone. "And I decided to do the same if I had to opportunity. And I knew that I would have the opportunity, Granddaughter, because every time I was taken to that room I was unchained. The people who jumped into the water were also unchained. When they would take us to the top of the boat to jump around like we were dancing, we were unchained. That's when these poor souls jumped knowing when they did that the man-eating fish were following the boat."

Maleka looks fondly at her granddaughter. "Would you like something to drink? I have some fresh goats milk?"

The girl shakes her head no. She then cups her hands together and rests her face, constantly staring at Maleka.

She continues. "Now, this is the part of my story that your grandfather did not believe, and when he began to tell me I was out of my mind. This is the part of the story that people say was not true. They say I made it up. That it didn't happen." Maleka leans forward in order to be a little closer to the little girl. "For a long time I did not remember what happened. I did not know how I made it back to the shore of my homeland." Again, she pauses to draw in a deep breath and slowly release it.

"But after your mother's birth, the horror of what happened came to me in a dream. Every night I was filled with the same terrible dream. Every night! Every night! Soon I was filled with every living moment of what took place." Tears fill Maleka's eyes and her voice chokes up. "I can understand why your grandfather left me, but he hurt me terribly when he took your mother and my other two children from me. That was more painful than to be called crazy." She pauses to gain her composure. She doesn't want the child to see her cry.

She needs a break from telling the story. "You look a lot like your mother. Does she know you're here?"

The little girl nods her head no.

"Do you want me to tell you the rest of the story?"

She now nods yes.

"Every time I went to that dreadful room, a man would walk with me. He would usually walk a little behind me always pushing me along. To get to the room we had to go to the top of the boat, then go down to a cleaner, fresher part of the boat. For a brief moment I could see the water all around and the far away sky above. One night when they were taking me to this terrible man, I decided to jump when we got to that opening." She smiles.

"Finally, the time was right and I jumped. I felt like I was reaching for the sky as I soared through the air. The next thing

I knew I was swallowed by the water, going down, down, down! And then I came up. It was pitch black down there and there was nothing but water all around. I was not afraid. I felt relieved even though I knew I was going to die. But I knew that my soul would remain in Africa if I died that close to the homeland."

Once again Maleka pauses, cups her hands together and holds them up high in the air. For a moment she closes her eyes. She then brings them down and looks back at her granddaughter.

"I couldn't swim. I had never learned how. The boat was moving off and I was kicking and splashing the water with my arms. I felt I was about to drown."

Maleka flings her arms high in the air.

"And then it happened. A barking fish came up to me and I calmed down. I don't know why, I just did. The fish seemed to tell me to get on its back. At first, I kept sliding off, but somehow, I managed to climb on. The fish swam off with me holding on. For days that fish carried me over the waters. Every so often, the fish would make its barking sound as if it were talking to me. Telling me everything was all right. Everything was just fine." She finally brings her arms back down and relaxes on the stool.

"When the villagers found me on the shore, I was later told that there was a great big fish in the shallow part of the water. They said they caught it and had a great feast. I was saddened when the fish was eaten. That was my miracle fish. Every night I pray blessings to it. That fish saved my life."

Maleka is absorbed in her own emotional rush. She remains silent for a few moments and then says. "That is how I came back. When I finally remembered what happened to me, I told your grandfather. And I told other villagers. I told anyone willing to listen. No one believed me, but that is the truth."

Maleka looks closely at her granddaughter. "Do you believe my story?"

"I think so," her granddaughter says. "Yes, I believe your story."

"Do you think I'm crazy?"

The little girl shakes her head no.

"Will you come back to visit me again?"

She smiles, nods her head yes, then jumps up, and runs out the door.

Maleka also smiles as the young girl runs off. It was the warmest smile she has received in years.

Sunshine and the Gummy Man

Sunshine was a slave. Now you might wonder why Sunshine was called Sunshine. Well, he was called Sunshine because he was happy all the time. No, he wasn't happy because he was a slave. He would love to be a free man. Who wouldn't? To be a free man was his greatest wish, his deepest hope, and his most powerful dream. No. Sunshine wasn't happy because he was a slave. He was happy because he didn't do any work.

You see, he was always trickafyin,' always goofadoin.' When old master would say, "Sunshine, go hitch up the mule to the plow, we goin' to do some plowin' today."

Sunshine would go to the barn and come back without the mule and without the plow and tell old master, "Can't hitch up the mule to the plow. The mule is sick and the plow is broke." He was always trickafyin,' always goofadoin.'

Another time old master would say, "Sunshine, go get the cotton sacks. We goin' to pick some cotton today."

Sunshine would go to the barn and get the cotton sacks and show them to old master.

"Can't do no cotton pickin' with these sacks. Some rats chewed the bottoms out of all the sacks." He was always trickafyin,' always goofadoin.'

On another time old master would say, "Sunshine, go get the hoe. We goin' cut the weeds from around the collard greens."

Sunshine would go to the barn, bring back the hoe and show it to old master and say, "Can't do no hoin' with this hoe. The handle is broke." He was always trickafyin,' always goofadoin.'

Master got tired of Sunshine getting out of work all the time. So one fine sunny day he went over to the general store and bought some brand new cotton sacks. Ten brand new cotton sacks! And then he hid them in the big house. And the next morning, before the first crack of day, he went over to the slave quarters to wake up Sunshine.

"Sunshine, get up! We goin' to do some work today or your back side is goin' to be mine with this bull whip."

Sunshine put on his clothes and followed old master out to the cotton field.

"Sunshine, I want you to pick all that cotton before noon or I'm goin' to lay you out with this bull whip."

Sunshine looked at all the rows of cotton. There were a hundred rows and each row was a hundred yards long.

"Master," Sunshine said. "If I got to pick all that cotton before noon, I'm goin' to need some help."

"Sing!" Master scowled. "That'll help you."

"I can't," Sunshine replied.

"Why can't you?" Old master asked.

"Cause a crook got caught in my throat lookin' at all that work," Sunshine said, trying to make old master smile. "Master, if I make you smile, would you give me the day off?" he asked.

"If you make me smile, I'll give you two days off," Master said.

"What would you do if I made you laugh?" Sunshine displayed a broad smile across his face.

"I'd give you three days off."

"Master, you might as well set me free as to give me three days off. Think about how the other slaves would feel lookin' at me takin' life as easy as a blue jay, sittin' under a shade tree, and drinkin' a mint julep. They would get so mad and jealous they might start an insurrection, maybe start a civil war."

"Well, you ain't made me smile and you sure ain't made me laugh," master said.

"I was just about to do that. But first I got to tell you somethin.' You is the handsomous man I ever did see."

"I'm sorry, Sunshine, but I can't say the same thing about you."

"You could if you told a big lie like I just did." Sunshine broke out laughing. He laughed so hard his sides begin to hurt. He laughed so hard his stomach begin to ache. He laughed so hard tears came out of his eyes.

Old master didn't laugh. He didn't even smile.

The truth about old master was that he never smiled before in his life. Some folks claimed that a boll weevil bit him on his lip and got his jaws locked. And if he laughed, he probably would get a heart attack.

Master went back to the big house to get a nap since he woke up so early to get Sunshine up. So there was Sunshine looking at all those rows of cotton. And he started talking to himself.

"Self."

"What?"

"You don't want to do no work today, do you?"

"Sure don't."

"Self."

"What?"

"Why don't you run away? Run away to Canada."

"You know old master will be lookin' out the window of the big house and see I'm gone and then send the blood hounds after me. You know that."

"Self."

"What?"

"Why don't you make a dummy, set him in the middle of the cotton field and when master look out the window of the big house, he'll see the dummy and think it's you. But you'll be on your way to Canada."

"Good idea!"

So Sunshine made a gummy man from the gummy tree. It didn't look like him, but he knew old master wouldn't know the difference. And he high tailed it to Canada.

Long about noon, old master came out of the big house to see how the work was fairing. He walked up to the gummy man thinking it was Sunshine.

"Sunshine, what are you doing standing here? Get back to work!"

Of course the gummy man don't say anything.

"If you don't get back to work, I'm going to bust you side the jaw."

Of course the gummy man don't say anything.

"I'll give you the count of three." And the old master starts counting. "One…two…three!" Then throws his fist upside gummy man's head and he gets stuck.

"Let me go!"

Of course the gummy man don't say anything.

"I'll give you the count of one. One!"

Master kicks the gummy man and he is stuck for sure. He is stuck for sure.

Meanwhile Sunshine is running fast and running fast. He's running fast on the side of the road at the edge of the woods. He's running fast and he's running fast. He figures if he runs in the middle of the road, he might get caught and if he runs in the woods, he might get lost. He's running fast and he's running fast.

Suddenly he hears a voice.

"Hello there, Sunshine. Hello there, Sunshine."

Sunshine stopped in his tracks. He looked around, but he didn't see anyone. "Who called out my name?"

"Me. I called out your name," the voice said.

"I don't see anyone," Sunshine said. "Where are you? Show yourself. Let me see you."

"I can't show myself. Not until nighttime. I'm the North Star. When darkness falls, you'll see me. And I'll guide you to freedom land."

"How do I know you the North Star? Stars don't talk. Least I never heard of one talkin'."

"Now you have and I'm going to take you to freedom land. But you got to do what I tell you. You got to go in the woods. Don't worry you won't get lost. Just follow the sound of the blue birds. They will guide you in the daytime and my beacon light will guide you in the nighttime. So do what I tell you. Go into the woods."

So Sunshine went into the woods. He was running fast and he was running fast. When darkness fell, he saw the North Star and he knew he was going in the right direction.

"Hello there, Sunshine. Hello there, Sunshine."

Sunshine stopped running. "I'm listening," Sunshine said.

"You're going to come to a river. You're going to see a man standing next to a boat. Don't be afraid. Don't be afraid."

After a while, Sunshine did come to a river and he did see a man standing next to a boat.

"Hello there, Sunshine," the man said.

"How did you know my name?" Sunshine asked.

"The North Star told me your name."

"Who are you?" Sunshine asked.

"I'm a Quaker, and that's my religion. I'm a conductor of the Underground Railroad. That's my job. Get in the boat. I'm going to take you to freedom land."

Sunshine got in the boat. The man rowed the boat down the river for a few miles. Then he pulled up to the bank on the other side of the river.

"See that house over yonder on the hill with the light beaming in the window?"

Sunshine nodded his head.

"Go and knock on the door. There's a lady waiting for you. She's going to help you on your way to freedom land."

Sunshine got out of the boat. He quickly stepped up to the house and knocked on the door.

A tall woman with a stern look on her face opened the door.

"Hello there, Sunshine," the woman said.

"How do you know my name?"

"The North Star told me your name."

"And who are you?" Sunshine asked.

"I'm a Quaker, and I'm a conductor of the Underground Railroad. Come in the house. I got some food for you to eat and a nice comfortable bed to lay your head on."

Sunshine went into the house and there on the table was a fine spread of food. There were collard greens, black eye peas, and mashed potatoes. There was corn, fried chicken, hush puppies, and sweet potato pie. Dishes were set out to eat on and utensils to eat with and a big glass of milk to wash the food down. It was a spread worthy of a king, and Sunshine was having his royal moment. After he finished eating, Sunshine went into a bedroom and laid his head down for a nice restful sleep on a nice comfortable bed. Before he knew it, he was fast asleep. Before he knew it, he was being awakened.

"Sunshine, time to get up. There's a man outside sitting on a wagon with two horses raring to go. They're going to take you on to your next step to freedom land."

Sunshine got up, but just before he was about to leave, the woman stopped him.

"Take this blanket with you. You're going to need it on those cold chilly nights."

Sunshine took the blanket. It was a patch quilt blanket. Once outside, Sunshine saw the man sitting on a wagon with two horses raring to go.

"Hello there, Sunshine," the man said. "Get in the wagon and under the straw. We got some traveling to do."

Sunshine got in the wagon, under the straw and the man got those two horses moving. They traveled for two whole days, just stopping long enough for Sunshine to stretch his legs and get a bit of food and drink of water.

After two whole days the man said, "All right, Sunshine, you can get out."

Sunshine got out of the wagon.

The man continued, "Go in those woods yonder. You're going to see a clearing and you're going to see some people like yourself and some women and children."

Sunshine went into the woods and saw a clearing filled with people. They were sitting on the grassy ground with their meager belongings. Sunshine joined them.

After an hour they heard some singing.

"Steal away, steal away, steal away to Jesus." The singing came from inside the woods. "Ain't got long to be here."

Out of the woods came a woman. She was a stout woman. She really wasn't stout; she just looked stout. She was a big woman. She really wasn't big; she just looked big.

"Come on children," the woman said. "We're going to freedom land."

The people gathered their meager belongings and followed behind the woman. She led them back into the woods. They soon came to a stream and the woman started walking in the water. The people followed behind. They all began to sing together.

"Wade in the water. Wade in the water, children. God's going to trouble these waters."

They came to the other side and kept on walking. Hour after hour they followed behind the woman. Just before dusk, the woman stopped and said, "We're going to rest here."

The people pulled out their blankets. Sunshine was about to lay out his patch quilt when he glanced over at the woman. She was staring at what appeared to be a patched quilt with some peculiar designs. She seemed to be studying it like it was a great puzzle. He glanced over her shoulders at the patch quilt. It had designs looking like farmhouses and forest areas and bridges with long stretches of rivers running under them. High up in a corner of the quilt was a yellow star.

Sunshine wasn't able to make much sense of her quilt, so he lay down on his patch quilt and went to sleep on it. Soon after, the woman awakened him.

"Get your things. We on our way," she said.

In the night, the folks got their things together searching in the dark. Sunshine looked up at the stars. There was that star that talked to him earlier in his escape. The woman walked in the direction of the star. The people followed behind. Sunshine knew they were going in the right direction.

They traveled for ten days and nights. Sometimes they would crawl through cotton fields, sometimes they hid in old abandoned barns, and sometimes they slept under bridges. But they kept on going and going on.

Finally, after all the hiding and all the walking, the woman stopped. She looked at all the people and said.

"You all is in freedom land now. If you go in that direction, you'll go to Michigan. If you go to Battle Creek, Michigan, you might see Sojourner Truth. If you see Sojourner Truth, tell her Harriet Tubman said hello. If you go in that direction you might go to New York. If you go to New York, you might go to Albany and if you go to Albany, New York, you might see Frederick Douglass. Tell him Harriett Tubman said hello. If you go in that direction, you might go to Canada. If you go over to Windsor, Canada, tell old Henry Bibb hello and that we still fighting the good fight down here in the South.

Canada is the direction that Sunshine went. And when he got to Canada, he went to a private school taught by Mary E. Bibb, and he met a fine young lady and got married. They had ten children, eighteen grand children, forty-seven great grand children, ninety-five great, great grandchildren, and no telling how many great, great, great grandchildren. And all those greats and great, greats and great, great greats spread all across this land and became our ancestors.

Stone Gumbo Soup

The Civil War was over and three Black soldiers were on their way home. They were traveling through Georgia on their way to Louisiana. The three men were tired and hungry and they hadn't had a restful sleep in weeks. The only food they had eaten were apples from an apple tree earlier in the day.

But they were happy because the war had ended and they were heading on home. They had walked for hours through cotton fields, through thick trees and brushes and across a river. They finally saw a plantation mansion through a clearing in front of them.

"Look there," one of the men said. "Finally, a place where we can get some real food and maybe a bed or at least some hay where we can get a decent night's rest."

They quickened their steps as they hurried up to the mansion.

Now the only people on the plantation were ex-slaves. The master and the mistress had left when the Union soldiers came. Now these ex-slaves weren't greedy people and they weren't selfish people. But when they saw these three soldiers coming, they thought of when the Union soldiers first came.

When those Union soldiers showed up, they said, "We come to help you people." But all they did was help themselves to the people's food.

Then the Confederate soldiers came and they said, "We've come to help you people." All they did was help themselves to more of the people's food.

Naturally, when these poor folks saw these three soldiers, it wasn't a welcome sight. They didn't know if there was a small regiment or an entire army coming up behind them. They decided to be cautious. They decided to hide their food. They hid their onions, celery, carrots, corn, okra, tomatoes, and what little meat they had. They hid their food in croak-a-sacks, under blankets, in bushel baskets, and in old buckets. They hid their food as best they could. And after they hid all their food, they came out to meet the three soldiers.

"How do, good people," one soldier said. "We wonder if you good folks might have some food to share. We've been walking a lot of miles and we got a lot a miles to go and we sure are hungry."

"We don't have any food," the people said in unison. "The army came by and ate all the food we had. There's a town up the road. Maybe the town folks can give you some food."

"How far is this town?" the soldier asked.

"Oh, about thirty or forty miles," the people said in unison.

"We can't walk that far," the soldier sighed. "We're plumb worn out. We can't walk another half mile of a half mile."

One of the other soldiers spoke up. "I know what we can do. We can make some stone gumbo soup."

"Stone gumbo soup," the people said in unison. "What's that?"

"That's gumbo soup made out of stones," the soldier told them. "All we need is a big cooking pot. Anyone know where there's a big, big cooking pot?"

An old lady bent over, with gray hair and wrinkled tired skin, stepped forward and spoke up. "I know where there's a big, big cooking pot. In the plantation house. I used to cook out of it for the master and mistress when they gave their big hoop-de-do get together. I'll get my husband to help me bring it out."

The old lady and her husband, also bent over and bow legged, with sun cracked skin and only blotches of hair left, went into the plantation house and brought out the big, big cooking pot. They set it right in front of the soldiers.

"Now all we need is some kindlin' to put under the pot. Anyone know where we can get some kindlin'?"

"I got some kindlin' leaning against my shack," another old man said. "I'll go get it for you."

The old man, who walked with a severe limp, headed to his shack, got the wood, and brought it back and placed it under the pot. Placed it under the pot.

"Now what we need are some nice round, smooth stones to put in the pot," the soldier said. "Does anyone know where there are some nice round smooth stones?"

"I know where there's some nice round, smooth stones over by the creek. I'll get my little brother and we'll get them for you."

The young boy and his brother went over to the lake, got some nice round, smooth stones and put them in the pot. Put them in the pot.

"Now," the soldier said. "What we need is a bucket of water."

Another old man said. "I got a bucket of water in my shack. I'll go get it."

The old man got the bucket of water and poured it in the pot. Poured it in the pot.

"Now it's time to light the kindlin'," the soldier said. And so, they did.

Soon the wood was burning. Soon the water was boiling.

"Mmm mmh!" the first soldier said. "Smelling good. Smelling good."

"Mmm mmh!" the second soldier said. "Smelling good. Smelling good."

"Mmm mmh!" the third soldier said. "Smelling good. Smelling good. But it needs something else. It needs something else. It needs some salt and pepper. Salt and pepper sure will bring out the flavor, don't you all agree? Now I know you are some poor folks and you don't have any food to share, but I wonder if someone has some salt and pepper?"

"I have some salt and pepper," a little old lady said. And away she went to her shack. She came back with the salt and pepper.

"Mmm. mmh!" the first soldier said. "Smelling good. Smelling good."

"Mmm, mmh!" the second soldier said. "Smelling good. Smelling good."

"Mmm, mmh!" the third soldier said. "Smelling good. Smelling good. But it needs something else. It needs something else. It needs some onions. Onions sure would bring out the flavor, don't y'all agree? Now I know you some poor folks and don't have any food to share, but I wonder if someone might have some onions?"

"I got some onions," a young and beautiful Black girl said. And away she went to her shack, got those onions and came back with them, peeled and cut them, then tossed those onions into the pot. Put them in the pot.

"Mmm, mmh!" the first soldier said. "Smelling good. Smelling good."

"Mmm, mmh!" the second soldier said. "Smelling good. Smelling good."

"Mmm, mmh!" the third soldier said. "Smelling good. Smelling good. But it needs something else. It needs something else. It needs some celery. Yes, it needs some celery. Celery sure would give this stone gumbo soup some flavor. Don't y'all agree? I wonder if any of you poor folks got some celery?"

"I got some celery," a woman with very high spirits said. And away that woman went. She got that celery and brought it back, cut it up, and put it in the pot. Put it in the pot.

"Mmm, mmh," the first soldier said. "Smelling good. Smelling good."

"Mmm, mmh," the second soldier said. "Smelling good. Smelling good."

"Mmm, mmh," the third soldier said. "Smelling good. Smelling good, but it needs something else, it needs something else. It needs some carrots. And it needs some corn, too. Anybody here got some carrots and some corn?"

"Me and my wife," an old man with his wife standing next to him and the two looking much alike said. "We got some carrots and we got some corn. We'll go get it for you." Those two old folks, in unison turned and hurried off to their shack, got those carrots and got that corn and cut them up and put them in the pot. Put them in the pot.

"Mmm, Mmh!" the first soldier said. "Smelling good. Smelling good."

"Mmm, Mmh!" the second soldier said. "Smelling good. Smelling good."

"Mmm, Mmh!" the third soldier said. "Smelling good. Smelling good, but you know what?"

"It needs something else," a large lady wearing a red bandanna said.

"You right," the soldier said. "It needs something else. It needs some okra. Can't make stone gumbo soup without okra."

"No, you can't," the same lady said. "And I know where there's some okra." She hurried inside the big house, got that okra, cut it up, and put it in the pot. Put it in the pot.

"Mmm, Mmh!" the first soldier said. "Smelling good. Smelling good."

"Mmm, Mmh!" the second soldier said. "Smelling good. Smelling good."

"Mmm, Mmh!" the third soldier said. "Smelling good. Smelling good, but oh, it needs something else. It needs something else."

"What about some tomatoes?" a young girl no older than ten, said.

"That'll be fine," the soldier said.

So, the little girl, and her little sister went to where their mamma had hidden the tomatoes and brought them back, and then some of the grown-ups cut them up and put them in the pot. Put them in the pot.

"Mmm, Mmh!" the first soldier said. "Smelling like that stone gumbo soup we made a while back for General Ulysses S. Grant."

The people looked at each other and said, "They cooked for a General?"

"Mmm, Mmh!" the second soldier said. "Smelling like that stone gumbo soup we made for President Abraham Lincoln."

The people looked at each other again and said, "They cooked for the President?"

"Mmm, Mmh!" the third soldier said. "Smelling good. Smelling good, but it needs something else. It needs something else."

"I know what it needs," the old man whose wife worked in the plantation house said. "It needs some meat."

"Sure do," the soldier said.

"What about some chicken," the old man said.

"That'll help a whole lot," the second soldier said.

"And some ham hocks and some sausage," another old man said.

"Very good!" the first soldier said.

"How about some fish? We got some fresh fish just straight out of that lake over yonder," the oldest of all the old men said. He pointed toward the woods.

"Great!" the third soldier said.

So those old men got the fish and the meat and brought it all back. And with the help of the women cut it in small pieces and put it in the pot. Put it in the pot.

That food cooked and cooked. The smell filled the air. And the folks took turns stirring the pot. The young folks stirred and the old folks stirred.

After an hour's time one of the old folks said, "I think it's cooked enough. I think it's ready."

The first soldier asked, "Is there a place where we can all go and eat this food together?"

The lady who worked in the plantation house said, "There sure is. In the big house. There's a giant size-eating table in the grand hall. And it's big enough for everybody here. There sure is. And I know where the mistress hid the dishes and silverware. I sure do. And some of these lady folks can help me set things up."

So, all those slaves who had worked the cotton fields for years, and those soldiers who fought a war to help get them out of the cotton fields proudly strutted inside the plantation house and sat at that banquet table. They ate that stone gumbo soup together, eating from dishes and with silverware they only dreamed of using when in the cotton field. They ate till they were well fed.

After they finished eating, the old men came out with their musical instruments. They came out with their banjos, fiddles, and harmonicas. And for the first time in their lives, played music they could enjoy for themselves because there were no more cotton fields. And they danced and sang; they shouted and clapped their hands; they celebrated because there were no more masters and mistresses and no more cotton fields.

They celebrated, oh how they celebrated! They celebrated freedom! Yes, they celebrated freedom! They celebrated Frederick Douglass and Harriet Tubman and Sojourner Truth and John Brown and all the people who fought for freedom. Oh, how they celebrated.

They celebrated the coming generations. They didn't know we were coming, but they celebrated just the same. They celebrated Malcolm X and Martin Luther King, Jr., and Rosa Parks, and all the people who stood up for freedom. Oh, how they celebrated. They didn't know we were coming, but they celebrated just the same.

They celebrated Paul Robeson, Langston Hughes, and Barak Obama. Oh, how they celebrated. They didn't know we were coming, but they celebrated just the same. Yes, they celebrated just the same.

They celebrated and they celebrated. And finally, they decided to rest their bodies. And each of those good folks went off to their shacks, leaving the three soldiers in the plantation house. And those three soldiers rested their bodies also. They slept in the master's bedroom.

The next morning the soldiers were on their way to Louisiana. As they were leaving, they heard all the people call out to them, "Good-bye! Good-bye! And thanks for the stone gumbo soup."